DOROTHY SALISBURY DAVIS

A DEATH IN THE LIFE

Other Avon Books by
Dorothy Salisbury Davis

SCARLET NIGHT

DOROTHY SALISBURY DAVIS

A DEATH IN
THE LIFE

AVON
PUBLISHERS OF BARD, CAMELOT, DISCUS AND FLARE BOOKS

AVON BOOKS
A division of
The Hearst Corporation
959 Eighth Avenue
New York, New York 10019

First Avon Printing, August, 1977

Printed in the U.S.A.

WFH   10   9   8   7   6   5   4   3

For Lucy,
friend and abettor

1

WHAT AM I DOING HERE? What *am* I doing here . . . ? There's a fly upon the wall, how I wish that he would fall. A fly in Doctor's office? Never. A mote, a beam. There's a crack in the ceiling. It gets bigger and bigger every session. Twenty-one floors of psychoanalysts are going to come down on top of me. Julie à la Freud.

"Doctor?"

"Yes?"

"What's going through *your* mind at this minute?"

"What do you think is going through my mind?"

"That I've got skinny legs and no breasts."

"What about no breasts?"

"But I do have breasts. When I sit up and lean over I can see them myself. I often look. Is that narcissistic?"

"What do you think?"

"I think . . . yes. I'm very fond of myself or I wouldn't be here."

"So. You want to be here?"

"I want to be here because Jeff thinks I should and he pays the bill."

"If he didn't pay the bill would you want to be here?"

"Mother . . ."

"What about Mother?"

"I was going to say if he didn't, Mother would, but Mother's dead and I wasn't really thinking of her. Of you, I guess."

"You guess?"

"You."

"So?"

"I'm twenty-five years old."

7

"And?"

"I want to run away from home."

"Where do you want to go?"

"Out. On the street."

"So you want to be a streetwalker?"

"Very funny, Doctor. I want to . . . What do I want to do? I want to drive a taxi. I want to write a novel or a poem or a play."

"It's very hard to drive a car and use the typewriter at the same time."

"That's my whole trouble, isn't it? I want to do everything and I don't do anything. I'm lazy. I'm just plain lazy."

Silence.

"I'm spoiled and I'm lazy."

Silence.

"But I'm not really. My mother used to say there wasn't a lazy bone in my body. Only in my head. You've got a good head if only you'd use it. Jeff says he married me for my brains. That's a joke. But so's our marriage. I don't feel married. Maybe that's good. But I don't feel unmarried either."

"How long has he been away?"

"Let's see. Just after Christmas—three months. I hope he isn't trying to be faithful to me. Did you see his article in Sunday's paper?"

"What about it?"

"Crazy, a man like that married to me. I mean he's brilliant, right? Brains. With my brains and his looks, disaster. I don't really want a child. I want to want one but I don't. And I don't really want to want to, that's crap. Conventional crap. I esteem Jeff. That's what it is. A steam roller. But every time I get flattened I get up and walk away. I don't even feel flattened until afterwards. I could curl up right here and go to sleep. I am lazy. I'm spoiled and lazy."

Julie looked around at Doctor Callahan.

"Why do you look at me?"

"I thought you might be yawning."

The doctor released the brake to her chair and brought it to an upright position. "You may get up now."

"Is it time?" Julie swung her legs off the couch and ran

8

her fingers through her hair where it was pressed in at the back of her head.

"Not quite time, but I want to say something which I think you are waiting for me to say. I think we should stop these sessions for the time being, at least. Not necessarily today, but soon. Therapy is a cooperative process. It isn't an afternoon's chat. Not every doctor is right for every patient. I don't know whether I am right for you or not, but I don't think I am at present. I don't think any doctor will be right for you until you want to come to them, until you want to change badly enough to make the effort. I have been urging you—For how long? A year almost?—to get a job. It is the only real direction I have tried to give you. That is also conventional crap. But when I do something unconventional it is because I think it is the only thing that will help a patient. I have many patients I can help, patients who need me, but there are only so many hours in every day."

"You're firing me!"

"Call it a temporary layoff."

"That's great. Just great." The tears welled up in Julie's eyes. She fought them back, but they came anyway and she reached for a tissue from the box at the side of the couch. She waved it at the doctor before using it. "I might as well get my money's worth."

"I understand that you are hurt."

"You understand everything. Don't you feel anything?"

"I understand," the doctor repeated.

"Well, I don't . . . Yes, I do. It's because Jeff pays you, and you're worried you're not giving him his money's worth."

"My dear, I have no idea what his money's worth would be . . . to you, and it is you for whom I am concerned."

"Thanks for telling me. Oh, hell. Let me get out of here. Today for keeps. I don't know what I'm crying about. Deep down, I'm glad I'm free."

"Nobody is free, Julie. To be free is to be dead."

"Oh, boy . . . Hey, you called me Julie. For all these long months I've been praying. Let her say my name. Let me hear if she knows it even."

"There is good reason."

9

"But you never tell me the reason."

"Finding out the reasons for yourself is part of therapy. When you decide to do something for yourself, and when you do it, if you want to see me again, call me and we will try to work out a new schedule."

"What if I find another doctor?"

The corners of the doctor's mouth twitched, the suggestion of a smile. She was a handsome woman with quick dark eyes that could sometimes be merry. More often they were the eyes of an observer, as noncommittal as the questions she asked in answer to questions. Her wit, like her wisdom, was under a tight stopper, but when she released it now and then it was to the veritable enchantment of her patients. At least, this had been the case with Julie Hayes.

"There are many doctors in New York. One of the others may suit you very well."

"Do you really believe that, Doctor?"

"I can be convinced of it when it happens."

"Me too," Julie said and blew her nose. She took another tissue from the box which she put in her skirt pocket along with the used one.

"You are recovering from the shock?"

Julie nodded.

"And was it such a shock?"

Julie shrugged.

"You are right. Answers don't always tell the truth, only what seems to be so at the moment. They are not as important as the questions." The doctor put her feet on the floor, a little looseness in her hose showing at a nicely shaped ankle.

"Do you ever wear slacks, Doctor Callahan?"

"Why do you ask if I wear slacks?"

They were both amused that the reflexive process carried beyond the couch and chair.

"I do wear slacks, and when I look at myself in the mirror, I think, What can you expect, sitting on your backside all those hours every day of the week?"

"You are human," Julie said.

"My dear, if I were any more human I would be a monster. I am going to leave your next regular appointment in my book. You may change your mind, but if you don't want to come in, let me know by Thursday morning."

"Thanks. Thanks very much." The feeling of abandonment and its consequent resentment were setting in again.

"And I am here in an emergency. You have many talents, I am sure. Prove just one of them."

"You bet."

The doctor went to the door with her, but neither of them offered the other her hand.

Julie walked a quick and random mile from the doctor's office, her thoughts swinging from one extreme to the other: She's right; she's dead wrong. She began to think up emergencies: *rape*, a crippling psychological experience, *sic*. Divorce . . . suicide. Which was so remote a possibility, it took her out of her despondency into fantasy. She had traveled from Central Park West in the Nineties almost to the Plaza, which, she thought, if she was going to commit suicide, would be a lovely place for it. She would check into a suite and say her luggage would be coming on later. "Coming on later," like from London or Istanbul. It was a phrase Jeff often used. Of himself sometimes. When he was home and they were to go to a party or a reception, even to the theater, he often sent her ahead with the assurance that he would be coming on later. At first she thought it might be a sort of training in "presence" he had laid out for her. He greatly admired "presence" in a woman (he was rather fond of absence, too). But now, on such occasions she felt like a kind of female John the Baptist sent in from the desert with news of the Big Man's coming.

Julie stopped long enough at the Plaza to use the powder room and there she remembered that she had intended to go to Bloomingdale's after her session. Her subconscious no doubt had pointed her that way from the time she left the doctor's. Damn her subconscious. It was her conscious that needed the hypo, her consciousness. What kind of a job could she get that wouldn't horrify Jeff? My wife the waitress, my wife the check-out girl at Gristede's, my wife the Revlon demonstrator . . . The job is for you, not for Jeff. The job, if the truth be told, would be for Doctor Callahan.

While she waited for the light to change on Fifth Avenue she watched a man handing out flyers. He peeled off one

after another with such a graceful twist of the wrist you'd
have thought he was scattering rose petals. Marcel Marceau.
When he came to her she said, "It's great, the way you pass
those out."

"You can have two," he said and grinned. Most of his
front teeth were missing. The smell of alcohol was pungent.
She looked around after him to see him looking after her.
"Tell Madame Eddie sent you," he called.

She looked at the flyer while she crossed the street.

Madame Tozares
Reader and advisor, psychic extraordinary

Julie stopped and read:

Are you troubled in your relationships with those you
love? Do you sometimes doubt that they love you? Do
you know your enemies from your friends? Do you feel
spiritually impoverished? Are you ill, lonely, afraid to
go home? Do you have bad luck? Do you feel that you
have lost your way? Do you feel betrayed? Madame
has advised kings who have lost their thrones, business-
men who have gone bankrupt, doctors who have made
mistakes, artists in doubt of their talent. No problem is
too great for Madame to understand, no problem too
small for her consideration. Madame will not hesitate
to give drastic advice if drastic action is required. She
will give you the wisdom to understand and the courage
to act.

"Oh, boy," Julie said aloud, folded the flyer and tucked it
into her pocket. Then she began to think of what Doctor
would say about Madame Tozares. Nothing so agitated
Doctor as instant therapy. She was a book burner when it
came to how-tos of the psyche.

Julie took out the flyer again to see the address of
Madame Tozares.

2

BLUE AND ORANGE. Royal, heavenly blue window drapes parted to show an elliptical sphere in one window and a Zodiac armature in the other; the front of the shop a waiting room with four orange-colored plastic chairs and paintings on the side walls which were explosions—or splatterings—of orange on chalk-white backgrounds. An electric floor heater also gave off an orange glow and heated the small store front suffocatingly.

A woman who looked to be in the final stages of respectability came out from behind the heavy blue curtain that hung over the door to the rear of the shop. Whatever Julie had expected, it was not a woman who could have been headmistress at Miss Page's School. She looked like money didn't matter to her, like the quick buck was anathema. She wore a smock over a lace blouse, the high collar of which was fastened with a cameo.

"What do you want, child?"

"Eddie sent me. Or do I have the wrong address?"

"I am Madame Tozares."

"Are you?" Julie said.

"Won't you sit down?"

Madame angled her own chair to avoid a direct view from the street.

"Do you wish to make an inquiry?"

"Well, yes, if that's what it's called."

"Are you in trouble?"

"That's what I was hoping you'd tell me," Julie said.

"Shall we have a throw of the cards, or shall I read your palm? Or I can read your mind, if you wish, and reveal your own character to you."

"I don't think I want that one . . ." She had almost added "Doctor."

"You prefer something more abstract, more symbolic?"

"I'd like to understand it," Julie said.

"That is why I am here. The Tarot is significant only if you understand and accept that in nature there is no accident, not even your coming here. Every event in the universe is caused by preestablished laws."

"Okay."

"I charge ten dollars for a reading."

"I guess I can afford it."

"You *know* you can afford it. Or else you can't afford it."

"All right."

"If I charged less it would be worth less."

"I understand." Oh boy, do I understand.

Madame rose and held the curtain for Julie to precede her into the back room, at the side of which was a partitioned area the size of a closet, bare walls, a small knee-high table, and two chairs. Madame indicated where she wanted Julie to sit and settled herself in the other chair.

She took the cards from a blue silk cloth and set them before Julie, a stack face down. She let her fingers rest on the deck. A fresh manicure. The long oval nails made her fingers look grotesquely long. "You will shuffle the cards by spreading them out and mixing them thoroughly. Use your right hand. Go from right to left in a circular motion." Only then did she remove her fingers, trailing them across the table as though there remained some invisible connection between them and the cards.

Julie shuffled as directed. The backs of the cards looked like the linoleum on a kitchen floor.

"Draw one card with your right hand and place it, face upward, on your left."

Julie chose and turned up the Star. Her next draw, under Madame's direction, was the Chariot, upside down. She was about to turn it right side up when Madame stopped her. Julie completed the five-card draw to shape a cross with Judgment on top and Temperance, inverted, below. That certainly seemed to tell her something just on the surface. Temperance was not her thing.

Madame took up the remaining cards, calculated the numbers of those open on the table, and hunted for number thirteen in the deck. She turned up Death and placed it in the middle.

Julie gave a little exclamatory moan, more than half in earnest.

Madame put the remainder of the deck back in the silk cloth. She folded her hands, rested them on the table, and observed the cards in a moment's silence.

She looked up at Julie with dark, brooding eyes. "You are very generous and you love many people, but you cannot love one person. Am I right? You have great gifts but you don't use them. Soon there is change coming. You are going to do something meaningful to you and you will be very happy for the time being. But there is weakness. You are restless. It is such a shame this fault in you, I could cry. You live with beauty. But there is something rotten, decadent. Somebody spoils everything for you and you have not the strength to overcome. You are married, am I right? To an older man, yes?" This time she waited for Julie's answer.

"You're doing fine."

"I am aware of that. He is successful, an artist or writer . . . something . . . is different every time he does it. He has a deep mind, a mind full of wisdom and advice on what everyone should do. He is not the great lover. You are his child. You don't have children. Am I right? He does not want children, you are . . . mixed about it. You are very lonely. So many people and yet you are lonely. Something has hurt you recently. Somebody has disappointed you, Not your husband, but somebody close. Your own family maybe. Your mother or father? There is something between that person and your husband. They are jealous of you maybe? They pull you between them like a tug-of-war. They are strong people. If only you were not so weak. But let us see . . ."

Julie knew she was looking at Temperance upside down. No good was going to come of that.

"Nothing works for you. You put the wrong things together. Is your husband going away? It will be better to let him go. There is separation. It does not have to be permanent, but it is very important what you do to change your life while he is away. You are going to do something which involves many people. They have great faith in you. A teacher, perhaps. Are you a teacher?"

Julie shook her head.

"I did not think so. I like people who are something. I like to interpret for someone who can go from here to there. You go everywhere and nowhere."

"How do you know that?" Julie demanded.

"I only tell you what I see. And I don't tell lies. I never saw such a mishmash." She threw up her hands in despair. Mishmash: that knocked out her Miss Page credentials.

Julie glanced at the cards: starting off with the Star, a spray of jagged stars decorated the card, stars to run away with, I'll come if you don't cry . . . Judgment peering out from above, looking like Jeff, the Chariot and Temperance upside down, and Death plumb in the middle.

"It's a mess, isn't it?" Julie said.

"Did no one ever give you such a reading before?"

"Well . . ."

"But you have a very long life and good health," Madame went on, not waiting for an answer. "And great love will come to you, but you will have to work for more understanding before it happens. Do you have any question you would like to ask me?"

"About whatever it is that I'm going to do that is meaningful to me—is that coming up soon?"

"Almost immediately. Many people are going to come to you. You may even fall in love with one of them."

"Okay," Julie said.

"Are you satisfied with the reading?"

Julie nodded.

"Is there any other question you would like to ask me?"

"That doctor who came to you who made the mistake—the one you mention in your campaign literature?—what advice did you give him?"

"I treat every reading confidentially. Every inquirer's fate is as sacred to me as the confessional is to a priest."

"Let's put it this way: I know a doctor who made a mistake."

16

Madame managed a self-deprecating little smile to go with the words "Send him to me."

"I'll do that." Julie took ten dollars from her wallet and offered it to Madame.

"On the table, please."

It was still there when Julie left.

3

JULIE FORGOT ABOUT BLOOMINGDALE'S. She went home and cleaned house, or the Temple, as she called it. It was one of those sober, useful occupations that balanced the scales of justice against the weight of her indolence. The apartment on West Seventeenth Street, mid-block between Fifth and Sixth Avenues, was the second floor of a turn-of-the-century townhouse. The ceilings throughout the building were high, the staircase curved, the floors parquet, and the windows tall and deeply set with inside shutters. Julie had a his and her feeling about the apartment, but not in a resentful way; there were simply rooms in which she felt more comfortable than she did in others. Nor, of course, did Jeff set any part of their home off limits to her.

He had lived there with his first wife, a portrait artist. Her painting of him hung over the marble fireplace in the front room which was called the parlor. It was a formal room with a fawn-colored Chinese rug and Victorian furniture, all genuine pieces. The *objets d'art* each had a history, heavy at the point at which it had come into Jeff's possession. He kept a fastidious journal of discovery, pursuit, and acquisition. It was a room Julie attended carefully. She sometimes walked through it as though to see if anything were out of place, but she never sat down there unless Jeff was home. She could not remember when it was that she first said of the portrait, looking up at it as she passed beneath, "That's my last duchess painted on the wall." Now the words had become inescapable every time she saw or thought of it. Many a session with Doctor had turned on the subject. Do I think myself as the next duchess? The last duchess? Or is Jeff the duchess?

18

Looking up at him after her reading with Madame To-zares, she did see a resemblance to Judgment and wondered what her fortune would have read if that key had been up-side down. But of course that could not have happened if everything in nature followed a law. Change . . . involved with many people.

A play? She had studied acting. She was a member of the Actors Forum. With luck an audience meant many people. She studied acting but she was a lousy actor. On stage. She had studied writing, but she was a lousy writer. On paper. She had studied psychology and all that did was screw up her relationship with people she had got along with per-fectly well until she began to understand them. Clinically. Operating naturally she was pretty good at everything. It was going professional that blocked her talent. Something meaningful which involves many people who have great faith . . . Hey!

Julie phoned Anne Briscoe and begged off a dinner party she had agreed to attend that night. She was about to go into her excuse, a medical reason she proposed to make up as she went along. Unnecessary.

"Now, darling, we're going to miss you, but it happens Allen Wiseman can't come either, so I'll just have to put his partner with your partner and we'll come out even. How's Jeff?"

"Great."

"Tell him we all miss him, but he's doing a marvelous job."

"I'll tell him you said that."

"I bet you miss him terribly."

"Like my right breast."

"Good Gawd. He'd better come home soon." Anne laughed falsely. "There goes the doorbell. I better see who it is before somebody else lets them in. I don't know why people do that with all the stories nowadays. I'll be in touch, Janet."

"You bet," Julie said and hung up. Who in hell was Janet? I'll be in touch. Okay. Good luck, Janet, whoever you are.

Julie went through the parlor again to look at the sky. She could see the sky out the back windows too. But out of them she could also look across the scraggly garden to a factory where rows of women sat over humming sewing machines from eight to five with no time off for good behavior. Or else months off. The silent, sheeted machines were even more depressing. The sky was a hazy blue. The weatherman was nuts.

At the Sheridan Square Library Julie borrowed a book on the Tarot. She read it over a dinner of shish kebab and Greek salad at Gus's Corner. The place was almost empty; most of Gus's customers took their kebabs on a stick through the open window, still spitting hot from the charcoal grill.

"Today you have *Finikia*," Gus said when she was on the last kebab.

"I was going to skip dessert."

"Have."

"Okay, I'll have." There were times when Gus said, Don't.

Gus brought the cake and two tiny cups of coffee. He sat down opposite her, uninvited—he never had been invited but he always accepted when it wasn't busy—and lit a cigarette. He wiped his fingers on the front of his apron and turned the book to where he could see it. "You believe in that shit?"

"Why not?"

He shook his head and then shrugged as he changed his mind. "Why not? My ancestors used to go to the oracle, the shrine, you know?"

"Delphi."

"Delphi, Dodina, Olympus . . ."

"Hey!"

"You think I'm an ignorant Greek? I'm a god. That grill—it's a vestal flame that burns there. I'm fresh out of virgins."

"Who isn't?"

"Is true." He took a sip of the sweet coffee, got up, and brought two glasses of ice water. "Are you going to tell fortunes?"

"Maybe."

"You wear a . . ." He mimed a complicated headdress.

"A fez."

"No fez—when a woman wears a fez—bad luck. A veil—mysterious—deep thoughts."

"That's too much hokum."

20

"Hokum, fokum. You could make a buck."

Julie took a bite of the honey-dipped cake. "It's great."

"Them goddamned Italians. They know what's good, huh? *Finikia*, you know what that means? It means Venice. That's where it came from. Venice to Greece to Sullivan Street." He got up. "You got the Tarot cards already?"

"Not yet. I'm just thinking about it."

Gus grinned. "First you should get somebody to tell your fortune."

"Very funny."

"You want to know where to buy such cards?"

"Okay."

"I got a friend. I will write his name down for you on Eighth Avenue. He's got a shop. Everything. You tell him Gus is your friend. How's the big newspaperman?"

"Fine."

"He's out there somewhere else?"

"Cairo." She wasn't sure. Last week it was Cairo.

"He don't ever like to come to Gus's Corner, right? Too many flies, he said last summer. In Egypt he don't mind the flies. How come?"

"You tell me, Gus."

The Tarot wasn't something you could master overnight, Julie discovered. Not by reading a single book, especially without the cards. What did happen, her reading set up a chain reaction: she went again and again to the books in Jeff's own library, *their* own library. Jeff always said every book she read automatically became hers as well as his. He had a considerable collection on the occult; it ran more to the origins of beliefs and their webbing into both social and artistic fabrics than to formulas for practice. Which was great. She was learning something new, and since it had no practical use whatsoever, she learned more quickly.

Toward midnight she remembered that she ought to write her weekly letter to Jeff. She turned on the radio and lit a cigarette. The music was wild, coming up from a muted drumbeat. She started her letter: "I've been reading about the Great Zoroaster in OUR library. *Zoroaster and His World* by Ernest Herzfeld, and, Jeff, the funniest thing just happened. I turned on the radio and what do you think was playing? a pop version of *Thus Spake Zarathustra*, which, as you know, is another name for Zoroaster. Crazy, but somebody really dug those drums. You'd hate it. I kind of like it. It's like pulling the old man's beard. But how's that for coincidence? Me telling you what I was reading, and somebody out there spinning platters tuned in on the same subject. I didn't go to the Briscoe dinner party tonight. Don't worry. I phoned and said all the right things. Anne said to tell you you were doing marvelously. Doctor Callahan read your Sunday article too, I think . . ."

Doctor Callahan: Julie decided not to tell Jeff about the therapy hiatus until the next letter. About Madame Tozares maybe never . . . Tozares: Z-o-r-o-a-s-t-e-r. Hey!

4

THE WEST FORTIES had been a kind of home away from home for Julie. In the two years she had tried to make it as an actress, much of her life centered around the Actors Forum which was headquartered in a desanctified church. She thought she might stop by there after visiting Mr. Kanakas and see what was on the bulletin board. Or who. Some of her best friends were actors. And some were ordinary people who still lived in the neighborhood where they had grown up. They walked dogs, shopped at the market stalls on Ninth Avenue, and raised plants on the window sills. You could see these people in the daytime, even on Eighth Avenue, with their shopping carts and prayer beads. The older women almost all wore hats. If they came out at all at night, they got lost among the shady traffic, the highs and lows on drugs and alcohol, the whores and pimps, the "porn" shills and their customers. Julie had never been afraid there, night or day, though a lot of people told her that she should be. But then there were not many places where she was afraid. In blue jeans and sneakers and her old raincoat, a scarf around her head, which was her habitual garb, when Jeff was away—except on her trips to Doctor—she was not a likely cop to any pimp, nor worth the risk to a mugger.

She greeted Mary Ryan where the woman was tying up her dog on the fireplug opposite a fish store.

"Julie, is it? I've missed you lately. Have you been out with a play, love?"

She was tempted to say she had been and to make up an adventure. Mrs. Ryan had ushered for years at the Martin Beck Theater. "Just busy."

"Say hello to Fritzie. We lost his brother last winter, did

23

you know? It's been terrible lonesome. I don't know what I'll do if anything happens to this one." To Fritzie, who was vaguely dachshund, she said, "You remember Julie.'

"Hi, Fritzie."

He was about as interested in her as was Anne Briscoe.

"Will you come up and have a nice cup of tea with me? Do you remember Mrs. Monahan? She was the one who read our tea leaves for us?"

"I do remember her."

"She's dead, poor soul. She was getting daft at the end, saying she had to get a chop for Michael's supper and him dead and gone before I ever knew her. Will I walk you as far as the actors' place?"

"I have to stop first at Mr. Kanakas's." Julie nodded toward the shop a couple of doors away. Dead and gone. Dead was not enough for some people.

Mrs. Ryan tucked a stray wisp of gray hair back under her hat. "Do you know, I've always wanted to go in there but there never seemed to be a good excuse. Do you mind if I come with you?"

What could she say? "Why not?"

"Will you stay here and behave yourself for a few minutes?" Mrs. Ryan said to the dog.

Mr. Kanakas dealt in everything from theatrical makeup to ancient coins to magicians' supplies. The place smelled of damp cloth and dye. An old man with the look of a tired eagle came halfway to meet them. His nose drooped down between enormous moustaches.

"Mr. Kanakas? A friend of mine—Gus on Sullivan Street —said you could help me. I'm looking for a good deck of Tarot cards."

"Ask for the Marseilles. They're the most interesting," Mrs. Ryan whispered.

"This is my friend Mrs. Ryan."

"I know Mrs. Ryan. Two dogs." He said it with the air of an offended person.

"Only one now. His brother died."

"My condolences. The good Marseilles deck is hard to find. You are lucky, Miss. I have one." He brought a paper bag and tore it open. The cards were wrapped in a faded

24

yellow silk cloth. "If you knew the history of these you could write a book." He cleared a place on top of the counter and wiped it with his sleeve. "Help yourself."

The cards were worn and frayed at the edges, the backs yellowed from what might have been centuries of use. The faces had that old look of dwarfs.

"Aren't they interesting?" Mrs. Ryan ventured. "I prefer old cards myself."

"How much, Mr. Kanakas?"

"You're a friend of Gus, you can have them for twelve dollars."

"Twelve dollars!" Mrs. Ryan said. "You can hardly see the faces on some of them."

"I was thinking of ten dollars at the most," Julie said.

"Take them," Kanakas said with a great sigh. Then: "Maybe I got something else you would like to see. A crystal ball? I got a friend, a cop, you know? When somebody goes out of business in the neighborhood he tells Kanakas. There was this old gypsy woman on Forty-fourth Street . . ."

Ten minutes later, having collected Fritzie, Julie and Mrs. Ryan approached the vacant first-floor shop on Forty-fourth Street.

"It's crazy. Wild. It's like somebody up there had a hand on my shoulder." Julie set the shopping bag Mrs. Ryan had loaned her down carefully on the sidewalk. Crystal was heavy and the ball was real crystal. You could look through it and practically see the microbes crawling around underneath. Even Jeff would approve its purchase.

"I know what used to be here," Mrs. Ryan said. "It was a Chinese laundry for years and years. They're all going out of the business. It's the Communists getting the upper hand, making them think they're too good for it. I wonder was it the gypsy woman my friend Mrs. Monahan used to come to? There's lots of people like to have their fortunes told them now and then. It cheers them up."

Julie shaded her eyes and tried to see through the dirty window. There was a break in the plaster on the back wall the shape of a dragon. "What if the fortune's bad?"

"Nobody's fortune is that bad."

25

"Want to bet?"

"You can print up cards and I'll distribute them at the next Bingo."

"Hey, I didn't say I was going into the business."

"All the same. It would be a very good thing for an actress between engagements."

Between engagements. That's me all right, Julie thought.

"And didn't you tell me once you were writing a play?"

"I was thinking about it." She had told Doctor she wanted to write a play. Or something.

"All kinds of people. Think of them, with all their troubles. You wouldn't believe it if they didn't tell you themselves. Don't you see, they'd be coming to you for advice."

"Let's go back now and have our tea while you think about it. I'll take down the agent's phone number just in case."

While she rummaged in her purse for a pencil the dog lifted his leg and gave the door front a brief spritz.

"Hey, Fritzie," Julie said.

"That's for luck, dear, and I dare say it's the last drop he has in him."

5

"THE THING ABOUT THERAPY, you can't expect spontaneous combustion, right? I mean until you try to make it work, how can you tell?"

"I don't know, Julie. I'm down on shrinks these days. Not that I was ever very high on them. But I'm on a downer, period. I guess it goes with the territory."

Pete Mallory's territory was theater, particularly stage design. She supposed that was the territory he spoke of. Maybe not. Pete designed the productions for the Actors Forum which was where she had known him and where she had met him again that day. They were walking the block's distance to her newly acquired premises.

"Territorial imperative," Julie said.

"What?"

"I was free associating. I do it all the time. Sometimes the weirdest things come out."

"It ought to be useful in the racket you're going into."

"I don't think of it as a racket exactly."

"No offense. Most things are or get to be, one way or another. What are you going to call yourself?"

"How about Madame Allure?"

"You're in the right neighborhood, baby. Seriously. I mean if you can be serious about something like this. Are you serious? Or are you putting me on?"

"Well, you know, Pete, I'm more than half-serious. 'Friend Julie': how does that sound?"

"Like a Quaker meeting."

"That's all right too."

"There's a difference, little girl."

"Don't call me little girl. I'm not anymore."

"Honey, at seventy-five."

They arrived at the cleanest window on the block. It had taken six buckets of water, a bottle of ammonia, and a roll of paper towels. "Welcome to Friend Julie's."

"How about Sister Julie?" Pete suggested.

"Too much like Sister Carrie."

"Who's she?"

"You're illiterate, Pete."

"It comes natural where I hang out."

"It hangs out where you come natural."

"Don't talk dirty. And nobody comes natural anymore."

Oh, boy. Julie turned the key in the door. "We're going to get a blast of pesticide. We'll leave the door open."

"I do know who Sister Carrie was. Laurence Olivier seduced her."

"Too late," Julie said.

"That's what I thought too. My God, Julie, what are you paying for this dump?"

"A hundred fifty. The second month's free if I'm around long enough to paint it at my own expense."

Pete touched his fingers to the damp wall. "Paint is out. Did he say paint?"

"Decorate."

"We'll decorate."

"I don't have much money left, Pete, not this month, and I want to make this on my own if I can. It certainly isn't Jeff's thing."

Pete looked down at her with amusement. He threw back the swatch of brown hair that made him look younger than he could possibly be. "Actually?" he mocked.

"Jeff's my husband."

"Oh, I remember." Which Julie found odd since she could not remember any occasion from which he could draw the recollection. "Who said anything about money? Money makes me impotent. Let me tell you the way it works for me . . ." His eyes explored the ceiling, the walls, the window, the second room, while he talked. "I do all these great things at the Forum, for example. I materialize sets for them out of thin air. I work my ass off doing odd jobs for a living so that I can pour my creative genius into their crummy,

28

dehumanized crap. I keep hoping that somebody over there someday is going to write a play about people. All right. I do get the reviews: Why isn't he on Broadway? But I don't want to be on Broadway. Can you believe that?"

"Yes."

"Then you're the exception. Or maybe I am. And when I do get a job off-off doing something I like, I wind up twenty-five bucks in the red which I have to pay out of my own pocket because the producer is even more broke than I am. I'm supporting a habit, that's what I'm doing."

"Yeah."

"What do you mean, yeah?"

"Well, this thing about a habit, you're really doing what you want to do, aren't you? You said yourself, you get the reviews. Everybody says, What would the Actors Forum do without Pete Mallory?"

"It's bloody well the truth."

"You've got things all your own way. Does anybody ever say to you, Pete, this set stinks?"

"It just happens the *grande dame* of theater said those very words to me last week."

"And what did you say to her?"

"Fuck you, ma'am."

"Even I know you got to pay for a trip like that, Pete."

"But I was right."

"Then especially."

He looked at her darkly, but the frown had no foundation. He grinned and it disappeared. "Who's complaining?" Then half-seriously: "What are you going to charge a session, Sister Julie?"

"Friend Julie. Five bucks a reading. Strike the word session. Five bucks till I get started."

"What do you mean, till you get started? You're already started. You must have been a con artist at sixteen."

"You bet," Julie said, but the remark hurt, no matter how Pete had intended it. Which had to mean it was something to think about. On her own. No more, "Doctor, this friend of mine said . . ." "So? What about this friend?"

Pete measured the walls and said that he was going to Dazian's that afternoon in any case. He would see what he could pick up in the way of material, something light that wasn't quite see-through.

"Do you want some money?"

"Read my horoscope for me."

"Okay." As though she could. Until she read the book. She *was* a con artist.

"Sagittarius," he said from the door. "In case you want to look it up."

Julie pulled on her rubber gloves and set to scrubbing the floor. A real con artist would have somebody doing it for her. From the age of sixteen. At sixteen she was a junior at Miss Page's School, getting ready to come out. Ready plus one. She had taken off that spring without telling Mother or Miss Page on a peace march to Washington and in one weekend had experienced pot, sex, and politics. After which coming out didn't mean even the little it had meant before. She chose her college and Mother decided on a different kind of husband for her little girl than she had had in mind till then. Everybody's little girl. Except Father's. Father was the con of cons, an Irish diplomat who conned the pope into annulling his American marriage. Look, Papa Paul, the child doesn't count, an immaculate conception. Or a Magdalene's daughter . . . Hey! What a title for a book, *Magdalene's Daughter*.

She got up and removed the gloves and went into the back room where she had set up the card table and the two director's chairs she had been on the verge of giving to the Salvation Army, they were so rarely used on Seventeenth Street. She turned on the gooseneck lamp and opened a new notebook where she made a first entry, the beginning of . . . What?

Pete returned with several bolts of shimmery green material and then went on to the Forum to get scissors, needles and thread, hammer and nails. Julie got a can of spackle and patched the major wounds. By late afternoon the walls were hung with a limpid camouflage.

"It's going to work marvelously," Julie said.

"I like the way you put that—it's going to work. Something that always riles hell out of me, and also scares me, is when people applaud a set before the play starts. How do they know if it's any good until they see the play in it?" To heighten the drama, Pete proposed to borrow a couple of floor spotlights. He demonstrated the effect he wanted using the gooseneck lamp, an illusion of movement.

Julie said, "No belly dancing in the aisle, please."

"Oh, how nice," Mrs. Ryan said from the doorway. "I've brought you a thermos of tea. You don't mind Fritzie, do you?"

"Do you know Pete Mallory, Mrs. Ryan?"

Pete remained on his haunches, but saluted the older woman. "How are you, Mrs. Ryan?"

"What a grand surprise, Peter. I don't suppose I've seen you since Laura Gibson's funeral. We do miss her so, poor soul . . . I dare say you do, too."

"Yup." Pete got up and put the lamp back on the table in the back room.

"That's a lovely shade of green," Mrs. Ryan said of the walls. "As soft as an Irish mist."

Pete said, "What's the latest disaster at the Willoughby?"

Mrs. Ryan lived at the Willoughby Apartments.

"You wouldn't believe the things that go on there nowadays. I don't know if you'd remember Mr. Bourke, the quiet little man down the hall? He was asked to leave." She laid a confiding hand on Pete's arm. "Boys."

"Shocking," Pete said solemnly.

Mrs. Ryan picked up the mockery in his choice of words. "I forget. Was he a friend of yours?"

"Is," Pete said.

"Well, you never know. Mind he's a nice enough man when you meet him." She sat at the table and poured tea into the two thermos cups. "I've had my cup. This is for the two of you."

"No thank you, Mrs. Ryan," Pete said. "I've got to go. I'll stop by in a day or so, Julie, if I can get the lights from Mr. Bourke."

Mrs. Ryan pursed her lips at the name.

"Pete, I do thank you," Julie said.

"You owe me a horoscope. I'd leave the front windows clear, except for a sign, whatever you say on it. Let all the mystery hang back here. The reception room's for the come-on. Stick a chair out there and see who turns up. I'll be interested."

"Me too. Come back soon." She stood on tiptoe and kissed his cheek.

A trigger response: "How about dinner tonight? Some come-in-as-you-are place?"

"I'd love it."

He said he would come by for her at six. They would return the borrowed tools to the Forum and go on from there. Instead of having to say anything more to Mrs. Ryan —or so seemed his purpose to Julie—he stooped down to pet Fritzie. The dog scooted away. "See you," Pete murmured to no one in particular.

Mrs. Ryan sat back and sipped her tea. Julie put the second chair out front as Pete had suggested and herself sat cross-legged on a newspaper on the newly scrubbed floor, the thermos cup in both hands.

"Now isn't that interesting," Mrs. Ryan said, "that he'd be a friend of Mr. Bourke's?"

"Is that bad?"

"Just interesting. I've never properly understood Peter. He's a very nice young man, but I do believe he's doomed."

"What's 'doomed'?"

"Well, he hasn't got on very far, has he, for one of the most promising young designers in American theater? They used to call him that."

"Don't they still call him that?"

"I don't know how long you can be promising, Julie, but I do know you can't be young forever."

"Yeah."

Mrs. Ryan gave that little pinch to her lips that portended a confidence not altogether pleasant. "Did you know he studied for the priesthood?"

The church was all around her. Universal. "It figures," she said, more in response to her own thoughts than to Mrs. Ryan.

"Did you notice? He didn't want to talk about my friend Laura Gibson."

Julie didn't especially either; she had only seen the actress perform once and she had thought her pretty awful.

"They were very close," Mrs. Ryan went on. "She would introduce him as her nephew sometimes, though I don't think they were related at all. In any case, he had gone to school to the Jesuits, and I do believe he entered their novitiate somewhere out in the Midwest. All before he got into theater, of course."

"The church makes pretty good theater."

"Oh, my dear, not like it used to," Mrs. Ryan said with melancholic fervor. She lifted her shopping bag from the floor to her lap. "I brought you something. I don't know whether you can use it or not." She dug out a cardboard sign: *Beauty Consultant*. "It belonged to my friend Mrs. Russo. She used to run a beauty parlor on Ninth Avenue. You could cut away the word *Beauty*."

"Or add *Truth. Consultant in Truth and Beauty*."

"There isn't enough room to say all that."

Julie got Pete's scissors and cut off the first word. It left a very naked *Consultant*. Ambiguous, to say the least. She punched holes in the top corners and suspended the sign on a length of heavy thread. Then, climbing precariously onto the arms of the chair, she hammered a nail above the window and hung it up. She came down to the floor face to face with a grinning black man outside the window, a white yachting cap pushed back on his head. He pointed to himself, to the sign, and then to her.

"Oh, hell," Julie said and motioned him away.

He shook his head.

Julie shrugged.

He started for the door and Mrs. Ryan came from the back room. As soon as the man opened the shop door, Mrs. Ryan said, "Sic 'em, Fritzie!" Fritzie set up a wild yapping and ran around and around, not sure of what he was sicced on, for the would-be visitor backed out in a hurry and closed the door. He made a rude gesture and disappeared. It took quite a while to convince the dog that he had already done what was expected of him.

Mrs. Ryan suggested that Julie ought to get a dog. Jeff was of the same opinion. "I'll take karate. Why don't you like Pete, Mrs. Ryan?"

"Aren't you quick now? Sometimes I do and sometimes

I don't. That's because he's changeable himself. He can be very abrupt. And I think he's queer."

"You mean he's gay?"

"I'm old-fashioned and I like the word gay for everyone."

"I'll bet Pete does too . . . if he's gay. I'm not so sure he is."

"Of course you are, dear, or you wouldn't be going out with him. You *are* still married?"

"That's right," Julie said. Score one for Mrs. Ryan. Half a point: Pete wouldn't have asked her if he thought something was going to be expected of him. Nope. Score one and wait for the next round.

Mrs. Ryan gathered the thermos cups and bottle. "My friend Mrs. Russo may stop in. She loves a throw of the Tarot. Her husband is a precinct detective. Fritzie, bring your leash, love."

Julie went outdoors with Mrs. Ryan and watched her and the dog meander down the street. She looked at the *Consultant* sign from the outside. It had but one thing to recommend it: it was so small you had to come up close to see what it said.

She caught a reflection in the glass of the black man in white cap swinging along the opposite side of the street in her direction. He started to cross and then danced back from the oncoming traffic. She remembered his parting gesture. For which he could not be entirely condemned, having had a dog sicced on him. Nevertheless, it was not a benevolent gesture. Okay, Friend Julie, confront. She folded her arms and waited.

"Thought I'd drop by again and give you a break, Miz Julie." He flashed his teeth at her.

"Thanks."

He wore a huge gilded cross nested in the hair of his chest, his shirt open to the navel. He flopped his fingers beneath the cross in case she'd missed it. The polished nails fell like drops of pale blood. "Just an e-vangelical call."

"Sure."

"What's a chick like you doing in a setup like this?"

"Like what?"

He screwed up his eyes and peered at the minute sign.

"Consultant. What's your main line? My name's Goldie, by the way."

"I don't think we're in competition, Goldie."

"I don't compete. My girls come to me."

"Lucky girls," Julie said.

"I got style, right?"

"You bet."

"Can't we go inside for this conversation?"

"I'm fumigating in there."

"All right. I'll buy you a drink while the place cools off."

"I'm waiting for a friend," Julie said.

"I'm a friend."

"An invited friend."

The smile turned upside down. "Don't smart-ass me, little girl. This is my turf and I just want to know who's setting you up in business."

"Me. I'm a marriage counselor."

"No kidding." The smile turned up again.

"Among other things."

"That's for sure. You don't make money on marriage around here. Unless you're me, if you want to look at it that way. I don't know what I'd do if it wasn't for the institution of matrimony." He touched a buckled shoe to a cigarette butt, nudging it into a crack in the sidewalk. "The old lady who used to operate out of here, you know her?"

"Only from hearsay."

"Did you know—I'll bet you didn't or you wouldn't keep Goldie shuffling his feet—she made her rent off'n me? A kind of referral service. A couple of tricks a week, it kept her going."

"That old lady?"

He gave a whinny of phony laughter. "I said referral. Don't you know what that word means? There's johns don't like to pick up a 'ho' on the street or in a bar. They think everybody's spying on them. So I figured a connection house, see what I mean?"

"You don't miss a trick," Julie said, not sure the moment she had said it that she had intended the double entendre.

"Julie, chile, anybody on the street's going to tell you, don't smart-ass Goldie."

"Okay, I'll remember that," Julie said. She did not want to provoke him, only not to seem intimidated by him. In fact, vaguely and very briefly, in view of the idea she'd had for a story, she thought of the connection's possibilities.

"On the other hand"—he started purring again and his voice really was rich and velvety—"you play along with Goldie and it's money in the bank."

"No way," Julie said.

"You're making a mistake."

"Could be."

He reached out his hand and tipped her chin upward. She did not draw back. If he had been a white man, she would have and maybe given him a crack across the face as well. Goldie knew it. "No hard feelings?"

"No." By shaking her head, she escaped his touch.

"You know something? If you were my girl, you'd be number one in no time. You could have class. It'd be a pleasure for me to take on the obligation. First thing, I'd want your hair growing down your back. You need a little silicon up front. Then I'd start on the clothes . . . I got a fifty-thousand-dollar dress designer on my payroll. I ain't bull-shitting you. Ask any of my girls."

"How did you find out my name is Julie?"

"I knew it from the day you bought the Tarot cards. If you'd looked in the crystal ball yourself, you'd 've seen a dark, handsome man coming into your life."

"No way," Julie said, aware that she was saying it too often, aware also of dryness in her mouth.

"I can wait, a gentleman of leisure. Any time you change your mind, just put out the word you want to see Goldie."

6

PETE HAD NOT RETURNED by seven o'clock, so Julie packed up his tool box and sewing kit, locked her shop, and went along to the Actors Forum. The door was locked, but Amy Ross, an actress Julie knew by sight, was using the wall phone outside the office door. Julie tapped at the window, showed her face up close to the glass, and was let in. Amy returned to the phone. She had not seen Pete since early that afternoon.

Julie went into the Green Room and read the assorted notices on the bulletin board. A rehearsal was in progress in the back room. A lot of Forum members wanted part-time work, according to the board, typing, baby-sitting, translating; several members wanted to share apartments. "Mary Ann" advertised herself as a good reliable maid. With references. The acting business was very bad. When was it not?

Amy Ross came through from the phone and made herself coffee.

"Do you know where Pete lives? Or where he works?" Julie asked her.

"They'd know in the office, but it's closed."

"I know."

"Did you try the phone book?"

Julie hadn't. Amy sipped her coffee and watched Julie turn the directory pages. "You're Julie Hayes, aren't you? Are you really psychic? A lot of the kids are into that scene."

"I'm beginning to think I'm psychotic." She could not find a single Mallory in the phone book. Finally she realized that a page had been torn out.

"Nothing surprises me," Amy said. "Not around here. No kidding, why don't you put a notice on the bulletin board? I'll do it for you if you like."

"No . . ." Tentative.

"What you mean is, put it up but don't tell me about it. All they can do is take it down."

"I guess. Amy, do you ever get propositioned by the pimps?"

Amy was lighting a cigarette. She scowled.

"I'm not saying you should," Julie amended.

It was the smoke that caused the scowl. Amy waved it away. "Every time I cross the street. One called Goldie, right?"

Julie nodded, relieved.

"He's a charmer. I always say, 'The Life isn't for me, Goldie. I'm as straight as a witch's broom.' And he'll say, 'What a waste.' "

"I didn't find him all that charming."

"He thinks he's paying you a compliment."

"Sure," Julie said. "I think I'll try Information."

"If Pete isn't on time, he isn't going to show up at all." Amy took a long drag of the cigarette and put it out. "I've got to get back, but see if I'm not right—it's Friday—Monday morning you're going to find a note from him in the mail, and if he's got money, which he generally hasn't, you might get flowers. Kiss-and-Run Pete, we call him, but he's a love, and he's got more talent than half the names on Broadway. When you leave, be sure the door locks behind you."

Julie got a number from Information, the address 741 Ninth Avenue. She got no answer when she dialed.

Julie spent the weekend getting acquainted with the neighborhood and dressing up the back room with small purchases from the thrift shops on Ninth Avenue: an electric plate, another lamp, a table with its legs cut down to make it coffee size, and a couple of folding chairs that had once belonged to St. Mary's Hall. As a child she had played at equipping her room with everything she would need for an ocean voyage, assuming that her room really was a seaworthy vessel. She pretended to be days at sea; she pretended never to hear her mother and her friends in the other part of the apartment, a thousand miles of the Atlantic between them. Even in college, which had been the best place in her life, she had been a loner. Or, more exactly, an occasional participant in each of the numerous cliques.

Pete did not show up. Nor did Goldie appear again at her door. On Eighth Avenue she saw a number of girls in fringe skirts and boots, some of whom looked like whores and some of whom didn't. On Sunday morning, a soft warm day, she kept pace a few feet behind one who definitely did—flaming red hair, a yellow satin blouse with a green vest, and a behind that bounced as she sashayed along. She was singing. A couple of boys made raucous noises after her. She turned and called out, "You should show respect!" and went on. A proper-looking young man shied away when she tried to stop him. "I got a little boy looks just like you," she said after him. Julie got close enough to hear what she was singing when she started again. Loud and clear: "Holy God, we praise thy name. Lord of all, we bow before thee . . . Infinite thy vast domain, holy God, we praise thy name."

All right. Julie crossed the street and headed for St. Malachy's. She proposed to attend what was left of the eleven o'clock Mass, slipping into a pew at the rear of the church. The priest had an awful voice. Someone she couldn't see from behind a pillar announced the lesson and began to read. A familiar voice. She didn't have to look, but she did. Pete Mallory. It gave her an eerie, uncomfortable feeling, as though she had seen something creepy, obscene, that she wasn't supposed to. Crazy, but she left the church as quickly as she could get out of it.

She started back to the shop with the firm intention of putting Pete out of her mind. If he had been more definitely in it, it would have been easier to get him out. She didn't even know what color eyes he had. She hadn't talked with him more than a couple of hours in their entire acquaintanceship. But they were easy together. She felt a kinship with him she had with practically no one else, a kind of respect for something underneath . . . Failure? "Money makes me impotent." It wasn't failure she had in common with

Pete, it was a peculiar kind of success, the kind most people would call failure. Including Doctor.

Gray eyes. Eyes that wandered after they had looked at what was in front of them and then suddenly returned, as though to surprise what was in back of what was in front. Pete had visions, she was sure; he could make anything seem beautiful if he wanted to look at it that way. So what had happened to her in church? What was obscene? It had to do with knowing he had studied for the priesthood . . . and Jeff. The instant she thought of her husband it was as though an avalanche of snow tumbled down on her, her mind a vast, closed-in whiteness. The connection had shorted.

Upstairs over the shop, a plump Puerto Rican woman was sitting at the open window braiding her little girl's hair. The youngster often played in front of the building.

"It's going to be an early spring," Julie said.

"Like summer. You had a customer."

"A real one?"

"She used to come to Señora Cabrera. I told her to come back later."

"Thanks."

"You should have a big sign in your window."

"I'm going to make one now," Julie said. She had brought the materials. Mrs. Ryan's *Consultant* wasn't going to pack them in.

Friend Julie
Reader and advisor
Tarot

She put on the flowered smock she had chosen as costume and having hung up her new shingle, sat at the table. No one came. She had lost her first customer. She arranged several combinations of the cards and worked with the Major Arcana following the instruction book. From its cryptic interpretations she elaborated with some pretty wild projections for her imaginary seeker. A couple of people from the Forum stopped by, a man and a girl who lived together nearby. With the need for practice, Julie proposed to read the cards for them.

"You first," the actor said. "I'm going up to Joe's and get a beer."

"Don't get lost," the girl said.

"Did you say *don't?* I can't believe it."

It was a weak clue, but Julie used it in her reading. Temperance followed by the Hanged Man: she suggested that the seeker was going to have to come to a decision. She was at sixes and sevens now because she suspected hypocrisy, deception. Without Julie's quite knowing when it happened, the cards themselves seemed to take over, and simply from her little knowledge of their basic symbolism, she found herself spilling out a stream of consciousness that held the seeker enthralled. It was an experience like none Julie had ever had before. A trip. A trance could hardly have been a less conscious effort.

"Are you satisfied with the reading?" she asked some five minutes later, a question borrowed directly from Madame Tozares.

"More than. Did anybody at the Forum tip you off about us?"

"That is very close to an insult."

"But you were right on."

"You threw the cards," Julie said. "Then they took over." The girl nodded. "Now I'd like some advice."

"Hold it. No way," Julie said.

"I'll pay you."

Julie shook her head. "Your boy friend's coming back for his turn. If I read, I don't referee."

"Him come back here? Are you kidding? He's gone for the day and good riddance."

"If that's how you feel about him, what do you need with advice?"

"You're right, I don't need advice. I need money."

"Remember the High Priestess. She seemed pretty cheerful about your prospects."

"She did, didn't she?" The seeker's spirits brightened.

Julie said, "I tell the truth as the cards reveal it. I don't exaggerate. I don't hold back."

The girl got up from the table with the attitude of someone on her way home to pack.

"If you're satisfied with my reading, will you recommend me to your friends?"

"You're in business, Julie." She went out wiggling her plump little backside. There was a smile under each buttock.

Julie was about to lock up when the former client of Señora Cabrera returned. She was a tidy little woman, pale, with a strained face. She wore a dark blue suit, good shoes, and carried a new leather purse. Sales personnel with commission extra, Julie decided. No rings and no marks to show that she had recently removed them.

"How much do you charge for a throw of the Tarot, Friend Julie?"

She was hearing that form of address for the first time; it sounded natural. "What did the Señora charge you?"

Her split second of a smile before she spoke didn't cover the lie. It exposed it. "Five dollars."

"I'm sorry, but I charge ten," Julie said. If she charged less, the reading would be worth less.

"I hope you're as good as the Señora."

"I tell you only what I see. I hold nothing back and I do not exaggerate."

Julie let the cards take it from there. Once, when she had been trying to learn a dance step, the choreographer had said, "Let the feet do it." She let the cards do it.

When the reading was finished the woman put her ten dollars under the base of the lamp. "I'm glad I came," she said. "I feel much better."

Julie went to the door with her. "Recommend me to your friends."

"I may," she said as though carrying something away with her that she was not yet ready to share.

"Do you mind my asking, Do you work at Lord and Taylor's?"

"Macy's."

Julie closed the door behind her and went to the back where she removed her smock and hung it on the bathroom door. "Macy's," she said aloud with wonder at her own perception. "I'll be damned."

True to Amy Ross's prediction, a note from Pete awaited

Julie when she opened the shop door Monday morning.

> Friend Julie,
>   I'm sorry to have gone into my vanishing act. A sick
> friend needed me and since that doesn't happen very
> often I stood by. May the gods inspire you and the fates
> send custom.
>
> Pete
> P.S. Thanks for returning my kit and kaboodle to the
> Forum.

So long, Pete, Julie thought. Disengagement. What an
exercise in saying nothing gracefully. Even his handwriting,
long and lean like himself, seemed to lope off the page. Kiss-
and-Run Pete, Amy had called him. Then there was Mrs.
Ryan's version of Pete. To hell with that, but to hell with
him too. Julie locked up again long enough to walk to Ninth
Avenue and buy herself some lilacs.

Later that morning Amy stopped by on her way to rehearsal. "See, didn't I tell you?" she said of the flowers.

"Yep."

The curious looked in the window now and then throughout the day, but as they would into a cage in the zoo. Ready
to run if a paw came out at them. A few friends came to talk,
but no paying customer. That afternoon Julie had cards
printed, thinking of Mrs. Ryan and her Bingo crowd. The
next day she decided to distribute some of the cards herself
to shops within a few blocks' range. Almost everybody gave
her a little counter space near the cash register. She was soon
on a first-name basis with the florist, the baker, the shoe-
maker, dry cleaner, deli owner . . . and Mr. Bourke in the
electrical equipment shop who had lived down the hall from
Mrs. Ryan until he was asked to leave. He looked so normal.
Square. A slight man of fifty or so with glasses that kept
sliding down his nose. He was very pleasant to Julie. The
boyish type.

"Did Pete Mallory speak to you about a couple of spotlights for my place?" Julie asked him.

"I haven't seen Pete lately."

"On loan, he thought maybe."

Mr. Bourke was accustomed to Pete's nonprofit business. "What did you want to use them for?"

Julie explained.

"I'll see what I can do for you."

"Thanks," Julie said.

Going out of his place Julie walked into Goldie. He'd been waiting for her. "Looking for me, Julie?"

"Nope."

"If any of the cats on this stroll give you a hard time, you tell Goldie." He grinned and drew his finger across his throat to show what he would do about it.

"You bet." She went into the fish market, which was the nearest exit.

Late in the day Mrs. Ryan came by with her friend Mrs. Russo. She left Mrs. Russo and took fifty of Julie's cards. Mrs. Russo represented cash, but what she was really paying for was someone to tell about the wonderful man she was married to, the precinct detective, and she inquired of the cards more for him than for herself. Something good was going to happen for him, Julie told her, although there might be a slight delay.

"Two weeks, two months . . . Does the number two mean anything to you?"

"Second grade! Detective second grade. That's the very thing I wanted to know."

Friend Julie became a familiar figure on Forty-fourth Street and environs, and people did visit her, though not by and large on a paying basis. Nobody could afford ten dollars certainly, and except with the Macy's woman on whom she had tested her strength, she would have felt like a charlatan to take it. She accepted five and sometimes two. She certainly had no qualms. In fact, she felt she might be doing some good for once in her life. And if she was not writing an actual story, she was filling a notebook with colorful characters, most of their color of her own invention. She did not miss Doctor Callahan. Definitely not.

7

SHE HAD SEEN THE GIRL before, a mere child. She had to be a child to take Julie for an older woman. "Ma'am"—that was something new in Julie's life.

"I need to talk to someone, ma'am." She stood with her back to the entrance. Every time anyone passed in front, throwing a shadow through the window, she averted her face.

"I read cards," Julie said. She was wary of the word *need*.

"How much do you charge?" The youngster kept looking with a mute longing toward the inside room.

"Come on in," Julie said and ushered her into the back room.

"Five dollars? Ten? I'll pay you whatever it is."

"Five is fine and you pay it later."

They sat at the low table. Julie could see the street if she leaned back in her chair. The seeker was concealed, and more at ease as a consequence. Julie still put her age at fifteen or sixteen, but a street person. There was nothing garish about her; she wore a dark green pants suit with a white ascot at her throat; her shoulder-length hair hung soft and richly brown, and her only makeup was eye shadow. Her own lashes. What was it then that marked her? And was the mark forever? It occurred to Julie that Goldie might have sent her, whatever pretext she was about to lay on: the thing about whores was that they were terrific actors.

"You know what I am," the girl said, getting it out front. She had no smile. Not for Julie. Down all the way.

"How did you expect me to know?"

"People can tell. Sometimes I think there must be a smell. I don't even wear perfume on account of what people say.

45

I don't walk like a whore, I don't think. I know I don't talk like the ones I know."

"Do you feel like one?"

"I guess that's it. It's when I get feeling like one, that's the worst. That's when I want to kill myself. I have a knife even."

Even. "There's a lot of them around," Julie said of the knife.

"It means something to me, just having it."

"How old are you?"

"Seventeen."

"Really?"

"Going on. I've been away from home over a year."

"They could pick you up for truancy," Julie said, trying to find some way to an up in the conversation. There wasn't any. "Where's home?"

The girl's eyes narrowed suspiciously. "No you don't," she said.

"I don't even know your name, for God's sake."

"Rita. Rita Morgan."

"All right," Julie said. It wasn't going to be her real name anyway. And who cared? "Why don't you just go home wherever it is?"

"I keep trying but I can't. I'm afraid to for a lot of reasons. What if I slipped?"

"Are you into drugs?"

"Not heavy. Pot sometimes. I get even more depressed." She was right. She didn't talk like the street. Not that Julie considered herself an expert. Nevertheless.

"How come you left in the first place?"

"Lots of reasons. Most of them my father. And I couldn't stand to see my mother crying all the time. When I went along with a girl friend that first time, I thought of Dad. There wasn't a girl he could keep his hands off. I think myself he should have been castrated."

"Before or after you?"

"Before. I didn't ask to be born. Not of him. Sometimes I'll see a john on the street and think, Oh my God, it's him. It isn't ever, but . . ." She shuddered.

"Look, Rita, I don't mind your telling me these things if

46

you want to, but just don't think you're going to get much advice from me, and I'm not going to be taking your money for it, I'll tell you that. I don't take myself that seriously. I mean if a person needs a doctor, I'm going to tell them. I'm not going to say I'm the doctor."

The way the girl's face screwed up, Julie thought she was going to attack her. Then the tears came and she pounded her little fists on the table. "I want help. I want to get out of 'The Life.' I wish I'd never got into it."

The tears were real and when Rita looked for Kleenex in her purse, Julie remembered the box beside Doctor's couch. It was not an office supply she had expected to need herself.

"Go ahead and talk if you want to."

"What I'm most afraid of is being blackmailed. I'd rather die than have my mother and kid brother find out."

She'd rather die than a lot of things. If she'd rather die.

"Who's going to blackmail you?"

"My pimp or somebody. He's a real blackmailer."

Julie flinched inside. Just like that, my pimp . . . my business manager, my agent. "Goldie?"

"Not Goldie. Goldie'd like to cop me if he could."

"Me too," Julie said.

Rita smiled. She could smile, and it was as though she had put on a whole new face, a Gioconda smile—something wispish, enigmatic—Oh God, there it was: something innocent. At the back of Julie's mind from the beginning was the question of how she had made it, a melancholic among the happy hookers. It stood to reason they had to pretend to be happy anyway.

"If I was going to have to stay, I might go to Goldie. I don't think I could fall in love with a black man. I just don't think so."

"And you don't want to?"

"No, ma'am, not with any man, black or white."

You're not telling it as it is, kiddo. What you really want is some nice young Bible freak from Iowa to take you in his arms and say, I wouldn't ever do a thing like that to you.

"Rita, what made you come in here? To me of all the people in New York?"

"I'm supposed to be on the street, hustling. In front of

Bourke's Electrical Shop. Sometimes when the cops start busting everybody I go in there in back."

"So Mr. Bourke sent you."

"Not exactly. He said you were decent."

"He ought to know," Julie said. "There's a lot of decent people and some of them know a hell of a lot more than I do."

"I don't know who they are. Everybody I know outside would say dirty, dirty girl. Or else go to the cops."

"You know the wrong people."

"That's for sure."

"What are you going to do when you go home?"

"Go back to school maybe. If I could just make it to college I keep feeling I'd be all right."

"You'd be fine."

"No I wouldn't. There'd always be a trick. I'd be standing on a corner maybe waiting for a light to change, and there he'd be—'Can I buy you a drink?' "

"You can say no, for God's sake."

"No isn't enough! I mean once he's said that to me, there's no other way."

"I guess I'm missing the connection," Julie said.

"That's because you're straight. I don't understand it myself, but that's the way it is."

"The only way to say no is to say yes? Oh, man, I don't dig it."

The girl nodded. A look of deep despair. She picked up her purse from where she had put it on the floor. "Thanks, anyway." She opened the purse.

"I don't want your money."

"It's dirty."

"No goddamn it. I don't know clean money from dirty. That's not what I mean either. There's all kinds of whores in the world, not just sex whores."

"Maybe you think prostitution is a good thing?" she said sweetly.

That was one way of fighting back. "I think it's a lousy thing to do to sex, to put a price tag on it. But people do, straight, gay, or in 'The Life' as you call it. I guess what I'm trying to say is I don't know a damn thing about it."

The smile. Then she reached over and touched the ring on Julie's finger. "But you're married."

"Yeah. Maybe that's what I mean."

Julie could think of nothing to do but to go to the door with her. She was angry and frustrated. If there was one thing she wanted more than anything else, it was to know, just to know. "Why were you scared of coming in here?"

"I told you, I'm supposed to be on the street. I didn't want my pimp to see me. I didn't want him beating up on me in here."

"Jesus."

"I can't stand it in front of anybody."

"Look. If you want to come back sometime and talk, just talk, it's fine. Maybe I can find a way to help you. Who knows? There ought to be some way for somebody."

"There ought to be," the girl repeated. She darted out the door. Once on the street she slowed down.

Julie went outdoors and looked after her. As she neared Eighth Avenue her walk changed: a kind of sashay with the heels taking more weight than usual. Julie tried to imitate it: it brought her bust into sight. There would be a real message in Rita's. As the girl neared the corner she took off her green jacket and slung it over one shoulder. Julie got the feeling of having been put on. To hell with her. About to go indoors again, she took one last glance—in time to see the girl fling her jacket in the face of a man. She ran immediately out of Julie's sight; the man plucked the jacket off him and took it to the nearest trash basket. Julie thought of trying to retrieve it for her, but before she had gone a half-dozen steps an old woman scavenger had snatched it and buried it deep in her shopping bag.

Julie went back for a dime, locked up the shop, and went to the nearest public telephone. On the stroke of the hour she called Doctor Callahan to reach her between patients.

"IT IS RIDICULOUS and inappropriate that I should see her,"
Doctor said.

Julie, sitting in the chair opposite Doctor Callahan, kept
imagining there was someone lying on the couch. "I'll bet
she'd say the same thing. Aren't you even curious, Doctor?
I mean, how many therapists get a chance to get an inside
picture of The Life?"

That little movement around Doctor's mouth. God forbid,
a smile.

"Why do you keep looking at the couch?"

"I keep feeling it's occupied."

"Why don't we use it?"

"Because I don't want to be at a disadvantage."

"Have you always felt that way?"

"No. But you said I had to do something for myself, and
when I just lie there and make pictures, it's not like that."

"Do you *make* pictures? Or do they come up?"

"Well, Doctor, I don't exactly develop them on the
premises ..."

Doctor cut in, a touch of impatience. "What about this
shop you've opened? Where is it?"

"Forty-fourth Street."

"What do you sell?"

Oh, boy. "I'd better try and tell it the way it happened,
Doctor. It was a kind of stream of consciousness."

Doctor Callahan covered her eyes to rest them while she
listened. Now and then she massaged her forehead, particularly the cleft between her brows, and every once in a while
she shot Julie a dark, incredulous look. When she finished,
Doctor said, "Why do you want to tell me about it at all?

You can answer that to yourself. I don't require it of you. I suppose it has occurred to you that you might get into serious trouble? That it might even be dangerous? Whores and pimps. What are you trying to do?"

"Get even."

"With me. Why? Because I want you to grow up?"

"Because you want me to grow up straight. Square."

"I want you to grow up. Nothing more."

"But there is a lot more, Doctor. I just can't find it, but I know it's there."

"The only possible advice I can give you, that any doctor could give you, is to close that . . . bizarre . . . that obscenity and do something useful. You infuriate me."

"That means you care."

"Of course I care! What do you thing I am, a robot? I care about all my patients."

"I know you won't agree with me, but in a crazy way, I feel I am doing something useful."

"Explain it to me."

"I don't think I can, Doctor. It has to do with hope."

"Hope."

"Yeah. This girl is sixteen years old and she doesn't have any hope. She hates herself because she's her father's child, don't you see?"

"I don't see."

"Well, I do. I mean I feel that I do . . . there's something."

"Is that how you feel about yourself? Are you blaming your father?"

"For what?"

"What do you think?"

"For abandoning me? Maybe. I do wish I'd known him. He was very handsome. And I identify with the Irish because of him. Mr. Ryan and Pete Mallory. I guess Pete's Irish somewhere. He studied to be a priest. I do like Pete . . ."

"Like?"

"I'm not in love with him if that's what you mean. But I'm not in love with anybody. I wish I were. Or maybe I'm in love with everybody. Hey!"

"How about this Goldie?"

"No. He's something else. Doctor, suppose somebody

called you and said, I need help. My name is Rita Morgan. Could I come and see you? What would you say?"

"I would ask who referred her to me."

"And she says Julie Hayes."

"I suppose I would give her the first opening in my book for a consultation. Then I would be likely to suggest a doctor I thought might be able to help her."

"Even if she said she was a prostitute?"

"This is quite ridiculous."

"I know, but it's real. If she commits suicide, how would you feel?"

"I would certainly not feel responsible. That is a sentimental luxury I cannot afford. I can only concern myself with my patients."

"But you work in a clinic."

"Also with patients. I see as many as I can. There are hundreds whom I cannot see. Furthermore, my seeing a patient—as you certainly ought to know—doesn't necessarily mean I can help them."

"They have to want to help themselves."

"There's a great deal more to it than that. But yes, that is the first thing."

"She does want to help herself."

"Then she has hope. She can take the next step and go to any psychiatric institution—Bellevue, for example—and get help. There are places for women in her situation."

"I guess. But it's an awful big step for as little hope as she's got left."

"Are you going to try to play therapist?"

"I don't know. I've got an ear if that's any help to her."

"And if this procurer of hers decides to beat up both of you?"

"I don't know. I just don't feel a human being can say no to another human being who asks them for help."

Doctor sighed heavily. "Give her my phone number."

Something began to nag at Julie on her way downtown: Had she made this enormous effort for the sake of a child-whore named Rita, or had she done it to involve Doctor Callahan? It was not until after she left the doctor's office that she remembered the doubts she had had while the girl was at the table with her. No, she decided, it was primarily for Rita's sake that she had gone to see the doctor; it was seeing that gesture of defiance, the flinging of the jacket, that brought her down firmly on Rita's side. Besides, if Rita was a phony, it wouldn't take Doctor Callahan ten minutes to find it out. It did not occur to Julie until then that Rita might put up an even stronger protest to the consultation than Doctor had.

That afternoon Rita passed the shop, arm in arm with a john, a middle-aged man wearing a Texas hat, passed right by the window, smiling up into his face. To hell with her.

But less than an hour later, the girl came into the shop.

"Hi," Julie said without enthusiasm.

"Did you see me go by?"

"With the cowboy, yeah."

"Do you still want to help me?"

"What did you have to bring him this way for?"

"So you'd see." She was wearing the green slacks and a gold sweater. No bra.

"I didn't need the demonstration."

"He wants me again tonight."

"Congratulations."

"He thinks he's in love with me."

"After forty-five minutes?"

"I saw him yesterday. I'll bet I could even get him to marry me."

"Okay."

"If I ever marry anybody it isn't going to be a trick."

"Besides, he probably has a wife and ten kids back in Abilene," Julie said.

"Laramie. He's here with the rodeo. He invited me to see the show tonight. If I thought he'd get trampled on I'd go."

"Great."

Rita walked boldly into the back room and threw herself down in the chair. She didn't wait for Julie to invite her. Nor did she seem to care whether or not she had been seen coming into the shop this time.

"Do you really mean that?" Julie stood in the doorway and looked down at her.

"I don't know. I'm telling you the God's truth, ma'am, I don't know. But I feel better when I say it."

"Have you got enough money to go home, Rita?"

"I've got some. I mean if I was going home, I'd want to buy presents for everyone, my grandmother, my mother, my kid brother." For a few seconds she seemed to be seeing herself on the way. "Sometimes I go to F.A.O. Schwarz and pretend I'm picking out a present for my brother. He's got a birthday coming up."

"All you've got to do is get there. Don't you see? They'll come running to meet you."

Rita shook her head, her eyes going dead.

"Why not?"

She was a long time letting go of the explanation. "What you said. They'd be so glad to see me."

"That's what you're really afraid of, isn't it? Not the blackmail or anything like that."

"Maybe."

"You think of yourself as a snail leaving a trail of muck."

"That's me."

Julie sat down at her usual place at the low table. "Did you ever think of going to a psychiatrist for help?"

"No, ma'am." Emphatically.

"Why not? If you cut your hand . . . suppose you were running down the street and fell, cut yourself, and got all kinds of crap in the wound. Wouldn't you go to a doctor and have him clean it out?"

"Maybe."

"What do you mean, maybe?"

"I'd go home first and try to take care of it myself."

"And if it got infected?"

"I do go to a doctor now. Mack insists on it. He pays the doctor for all of us."

Mack, Mac?

"All right. I've got a doctor I go to, a psychoanalyst. She's great. You wouldn't believe the things I tell her about what goes on in my head. Wild. I'll bet there's nothing you've ever experienced in The Life that hasn't gone through my mind. I mean I'm a walking porn shop, if you want to look at it that way."

The youngster looked at her, not believing. "Sex stuff?"

"You bet. I got an imagination that runs to gang rape sometimes. Sometimes I even think of God as one great big penis."

Rita's eyes had become little dark buttons. "You're saying those things because I'm a whore."

"You'd be surprised who I'd say them to if I thought it would mean something." The fact was she had not said them to Doctor. The fact was she had read the gang rape fantasy somewhere and the God part had just come into her head while she was talking. "I kind of like the idea that I've shocked you, if you want to know the truth. Sometimes I used to try to shock Doctor Callahan. But she caught on and she's shockproof anyway. The way I see your situation, little girl, little shocked girl . . . oh, my God . . . you *are* in a bind, but the bind is in your head, don't you see? Somebody who knows how to think straight and knows more about the human psyche than I do could straighten you out in a jiffy. Just by putting things, one by one, in the right place. What bugged you just now: that I said those things because you're a whore? Or was it because *I* said them?"

"It was that, I guess. I didn't think you'd say anything like that."

"What am I supposed to be? Some kind of holy woman? Well, let me tell you right now, I'm not any holier than thou."

The flit of a smile.

"Will you call Doctor Callahan and go see her? Just once. See what happens. You took a chance coming in here, didn't you? Are you any worse off than you were before?"

She shook her head.

"I'll write the phone number down for you," Julie said, and tore a piece of paper from the back of her notebook. She remembered the little box of cards, but used the notebook paper nonetheless. "Tell Doctor that Julie told you to call her."

"Friend Julie."

"Just Julie."

All the anxiety symptoms of the first visit had disappeared. "Where's your boss today?" Julie asked at the door.

"He's breaking in a new girl."

"I see," Julie said, although she didn't.

Rita knew she didn't. "It's kind of like a honeymoon, supposed to be."

"For goodness' sake," Julie said, getting the picture. She wasn't often shocked herself.

"Thanks for everything," Rita said, on the way down again.

"Are you going to call Doctor Callahan?"

"I've got to think about it."

"She's expecting you to," Julie said. Her last trump.

Julie had got into the habit of stepping outside the shop when visitors were leaving, a moment or two outside the walls and with a swatch of sky to look up into. Her upstairs neighbor was at the window. She often was.

"How is business?" the woman asked.

"Okay."

"You will stay?"

"Not forever, but I'll stay for now."

"Would you like to have supper with Juanita and me? My husband works late tonight."

Juanita came to the window, seven or eight, with dark solemn eyes and a mouth that looked as though it had been built around a thumb.

"That's very nice of you. All right."

"Whenever you close up."

At six Julie locked the shop door and went up the green-walled tenement stairway. She took with her a fresh bunch of tulips she had bought that morning.

"Our name is Rodriguez," the woman said and engulfed Julie's hand in a clasp that felt like warm bread dough.

"How do you do? I'm Julie Hayes."

"Julie." Mrs. Rodriguez made it sound like "Woolie." "Papa works extra sometimes on the ferry boat to Staten Island."

"Is he a pilot?" That was something out of Julie's own fantasy.

"Only up here," Mrs. Rodriguez said and tapped her head.

"Me too," Julie said.

The room was aglow with the light of seven or eight lamps and crowded with bric-a-brac and heavy furniture in plastic covers. There was a general feeling of cleanliness which was reassuring. A picture of the three Rodriguezes, the Señora in bridal veil and Juanita not much different from the way she looked today, stood on the table. Papa's main distinction was a mammoth moustache. A second marriage, Julie decided. The wall was hung with a picture of Jesus after open-heart surgery. The way He pointed it out caused her to think of Goldie and his golden cross. Mrs. Rodriguez removed some artificial flowers from a horn-shaped vase, put water in it, and set Julie's tulips under the Christus. Juanita was left to entertain the guest while her mother set out their supper on a table near the windows. In the absence of conversation, Julie suggested that Juanita show her her dolls. She had seen most of them at one time or another on the sidewalk outside the shop, not a one of them that wasn't missing clothes or an arm or leg. "Old friends," she said, and asked their names. That got them by until supper was served. Chicken and rice and salad. It wasn't much easier to talk with the mother than with the child.

"Señora Cabrera was like family," Mrs. Rodriguez said, and Julie hoped to God they could get a conversation going on that old lady.

"I wish I'd known her."

"She could teach you. Do you have good powers?"

"Pretty good."

"You will read the cards for me and I will tell you the truth."

"Okay."

"I am like a daughter to her, you know? Juanita, she tells everybody, her grandchild. Sometimes she plays for hours in the waiting room—an old deck of cards."

Julie felt she was being measured for a built-in baby-sitter. Something. "Do you work, Mrs. Rodriguez?"

Mrs. Rodriguez ignored the question. "People like to see a child. If their luck is not so good, a child speaks for something better going to happen in the future. They come in to find out."

She was being offered a little shill.

"She never interrupts and does what she's told. Five days a week Papa works for the subway. Weekends and nights he does the moonlight. He sends all his money home to buy a farm. I think his brothers steal it from him. He never knows, but if I steal it, he knows twenty-five cents."

Julie would have thought from the looks of the place that Papa was a pretty good provider. She betrayed the thought, glancing around the room. She didn't care. To hell with all complainers.

"I like nice things. You can see?" The woman smiled.

"Beautiful," Julie said.

"When you finish your supper I will show you the bedroom."

Oh, boy. That invitation to supper: Mrs. Rodriguez had popped it, seeing Rita come and go downstairs. "I think I've had enough to eat thank you. It was delicious."

Mrs. Rodriguez ordered the child to clear the table. She spoke in Spanish. The child obeyed like a mama doll. Julie was given the bedroom tour.

Louis-something-or-other-style chairs, a taffeta cover on the bed, crystal jars on the dresser. Just the place for Papa when he came up out of the subway. It smelled like a perfume factory.

"Very nice," Julie said, staying close to the door.

"You'd never know from the outside, would you?"

"That's for sure.'

"So we can make the same arrangement?"

"Hold everything. What arrangement?"

The smile slipped out of the voice and off the face. "I know the arrangement with Mr. Goldie."

"I canceled that contract, Mrs. Rodriguez."

"But that girl . . ."

"A friend and she doesn't go with Goldie."

"She's on the street. I'm not on the street."

"So?"

"Now and then, just one. Goldie never knows and Juanita stays downstairs with you. We go half and half. It is such a good arrangement. What harm?"

"I'm just not into that scene. I'm sorry." Sorry!

58

"Friend Julie"—the woman's lips curled nastily around the words—"I don't believe you."

"Okay. Ask Goldie."

"Don't smart-ass me, little blond bitch."

Right out of Goldie's repertoire.

"Thanks for the supper, Mrs. Rodriguez." Julie got out of the bedroom and found her purse.

"What did you come up here for?"

"To bring flowers to Jesus. Buenos noches, Juanita."

"Julie, wait. I do not understand, you know? I think everything is the same." The voice had changed again, buttery, and she closed the bedroom door behind her. "I will make us coffee. Good Spanish coffee."

"I don't think so, Mrs. Rodriguez, but no hard feelings. What you do is none of my business. I don't care. I don't judge, I don't care. Okay?"

"Okay. What harm?"

"I said it's none of my business. Only I'm not in the racket."

"If somebody comes . . . Terry maybe, and asks for Rose . . ."

"I get it. I'll say *you* still live upstairs. It's only the downstairs management that's changed."

"Gracias."

"Don't mention it."

"You must never tell Goldie."

"No, ma'am."

"It was a secret, Señora and me."

"What if he'd found out?"

"Señora Cabrera, she would take care of him. You don't have curses, no?"

"I'm not into that yet," Julie said.

JULIE WANTED TO LAUGH at the Rodriguez situation—a Rose by any other name—and hell, as the woman said, what harm? If Westchester housewives turned *belles du jour,* why not Rose Rodriguez of Forty-fourth Street, Manhattan? Julie hated her wildly and she liked the feeling, never mind what about it, Doctor. She hated her more than she did Goldie. And she hated the child with her mutilated dolls. And there it was: the child that was being mutilated, used, the silent, obedient victim.

Goddamn.

She took a long letter from Jeff into the bath with her and read it just above water level. He was going to Cyprus for a couple of weeks. After which he would be in Paris. "If you feel you can take the time away from Dr. Callahan, how would you like to join me for the month of June in Paris? It's time we had another honeymoon. I find myself missing my little girl very much tonight . . ."

"Me too," Julie said aloud. A reflex. Her me-toos were a cop-out. She could hardly remember the first honeymoon. What she did remember was the fight with her mother in the bedroom while she changed into traveling clothes. She'd rather have changed into blue jeans and sneakers and she wound up screaming at Mother, You go, why don't you go instead of me? You're more married to him than I am . . . something like that, and she was. She'd courted Jeff from the moment she laid eyes on him. On the platform at Julie's graduation from college. He'd got an honorary degree. Cum Julie.

Come Julie.

She tried a half-hour of Yoga.

When the phone rang it startled her. It hadn't been ringing much lately.

"Pete! What a nice surprise."

"I just met Mrs. Ryan and her goddamn dog. If he had more teeth he'd 've chewed off my ankle."

"I don't think he likes men. How are you, Pete?" She could feel her heartbeat in her throat.

"How should I be? I'm working with a bunch of stupid micks at the New Irish Theatre. They don't know a ceiling spot from the star of Bethlehem. How's the wheel of fortune?"

"Going round and round. Something new every day." He waited. Then: "I'm listening."

"Today there was Mrs. Rodriguez upstairs. It's a long story."

"I've got a pocketful of dimes."

She was tempted to ask him if he would like to come down to Seventeenth Street. But if he said no? "It turns out my predecessor had a deal with Goldie. Do you know who he is?"

"I know him."

"Friend Julie's Place used to be a way station, a sort of connection between trick and . . . treat. Hey!"

"I got it. Are you surprised?"

"I guess not really. But the lady upstairs—that's something else." She told him about Mrs. Rodriguez's expectations.

"Street games," Pete said.

"It's the child that bugs me, those great big empty eyes."

"Little Orphan Annie."

"Warbucks," Julie said. "Money is rotten, Pete."

"That's where we left off. What isn't rotten?"

"You, me, spring, poetry, hope . . . There's a girl that's been in to see me twice now, a sixteen-year-old whore who wants to go home."

"Sixteen," Pete said.

"Going on seventeen, she says. I'd have said younger."

"Did she tell you where home was?"

"No."

"So you couldn't give her the exact fare."

"Don't be cynical, Pete. It's not like you."

"Honey, what's like me? Do you know?"

"No."

"Then don't romanticize me. I'm not a romantic figure. I'm not even nice most of the time. Would you like to see the plays? Yeats—what else would the New Irish Theatre do?"

"I love Yeats. I would like to see them, yes."

"They make nice noise."

"When am I invited for?"

"It opens Friday night. That'll be a shambles. Come on Saturday. A few minutes before eight and I'll walk you through."

"Thank you, Pete. I'm looking forward to it."

"Take care."

He had only needed one dime.

She found herself listening to what seemed like the echo of her own words. Thank you, Pete. I'm looking forward to it. She thought of Mrs. Ryan standing on tiptoe in Mr. Kanakas's wanting to be in on everything, but careful not to touch.

Touch, touch, touch.

"Dearest Jeff, I'll talk to Doctor about Paris in June . . ." April in New York . . . April is the cruelest month . . . They had honeymooned on an island off the coast of Maine. They had bathed in the rock pools . . . two different pools, his and hers. After dark they had made love, retaining a certain anonymity.

10

JUANITA PLAYED in front of the shop so much of the time
Julie wondered if Mrs. Rodriguez wasn't psyching her into
the baby-sitting role in spite of the *cordon sanitaire*. She
often did find herself looking out to see how the child was
doing. Why wasn't she in school? Why, when other children
in the block were not in school, wasn't Juanita playing with
some of them? The child hauled a cardboard box bump,
bump, bump down the stairs and took her dolls out one by
one and seated them against the wall beneath Julie's window.
That solemn little face was always bobbing up and down in
the window as she went from doll to doll to punish each for
an imaginary wickedness.

Julie did more reading than writing, and a lot of watching;
she knew she was waiting. Five days had passed since Rita's
last visit. She avoided Eighth Avenue, not wanting to see her
there. If she was there. The rodeo was still in town, the trick
from Wyoming. Now and then a seeker came for a throw of
the Tarot, Friend Julie's card in hand. Always women,
bored, stuck, discontented women who wanted something
about which they were calling to do nothing. They came for
a fix. Julie had made seventy-four dollars to date. Seventy-
four. Seven, four, and one were numbers that often recurred
in her life. She lived on Seventeenth Street. Her childhood
phone number had been 7714, Rita was going on seventeen,
and Pete lived at 741. Whenever she doodled in numbers, it
was with a combination of the three. And on the first of June
Jeff was going to be forty-one, he had reminded her in his
letter. She decided to invent a layout of the Tarot, seven,
four, and one. At the moment it occurred to her to wonder
if Juanita might by any chance be seven years old, she

leaned back in her chair and looked out the window in time to see a sleek giant of a man stoop and roughly push the child out of his way. Both Mrs. Rodriguez and Julie responded. He looked up to the window above and down to the door, then up to the window again. Julie drew back without opening the door. He was a caricature, but of what? The cream-colored, tight-fitting suit with its braided lapels, contoured with muscles. Sulky good looks and wavy red hair that was almost orange, a dye job that must have curdled. He kept answering Mrs. Rodriguez back, his soft mouth curling into the shape of what Julie was sure were obscenities. Finally he took some coins from his pocket and flung them on the ground for the child to gather. He came into the shop, the scent of his male cologne like an emanation.

Julie waited, her hands fisted in the pockets of her smock.

He looked at her as though it was she who was ridiculous. "Are you Salvation Army or what?"

"There's a sign in the window. What can I do for you?"

"They call me Mack around the neighborhood. Now do you know?"

"I've heard the name," Julie said.

"I don't like Jesus freaks messing with my girls."

"You got the wrong address, Mister Mack. I don't think I could even call myself a friend of Jesus."

He sat down in the chair out front without being asked. Fine. She preferred to look down to him than to look up.

"How about Rita? A friend of hers?"

"An acquaintance."

"Where is she?"

"I've been wondering the same thing myself, and that's the God's truth."

"If it ain't, I'll find out and it won't do you any good, sister."

"I don't know that I'd tell you if I did know, but the simple truth is, I don't."

"That's twice you don't know. Once more."

"Same answer."

"She come to you, didn't she, saying how she'd like to quit The Life and go home? That's bullshit. She's the best

64

little hustler on the street, but she's so jealous of me taking a new girl, she cuts out every time."

"Well," Julie said, feeling a little sick, if this were so, at having possibly involved Doctor Callahan, "you know her better than I do." Rita had admitted Mack was breaking in a new girl. What Julie thought was something like disgust might have been jealousy.

"Straight people don't understand how my girls feel about me."

Julie shrugged. Then, on impulse: "How do you feel about you?"

"I like me a lot."

Julie just nodded.

"Don't understand that, do you?"

"That's right, man."

"The only way to dig The Life is from the inside."

"Goldie said something like that to me the other day."

"That man's something else, isn't he? Now if you was to ask me how I feel, a white man in a black man's trade, that'd show you understood a little."

"You know what, Mack? I just realized something: I'm not really curious. I don't give a damn."

"Then don't try getting my girls out of The Life, because you can't do it."

"I keep telling you, that's not my mission. Where did you get the idea it was? How come you're here anyway?"

"My girls take care of one another when I'm not around. Wife-in-laws, do you dig that?"

"Not mathematically."

"You're too damn smart, too smart for your own good."

"Sorry," Julie said. "But I would like to know where the idea that I'm into religion came from."

"Don't get me wrong, sister, I've got no objection to religion as long as it don't get in the way of business."

"Okay, Mack. It doesn't matter. If I see Rita I'll tell her you were looking for her. Okay?"

"Just tell her to get her little ass back on the street. I got a big weekend coming up and I need the cash."

"I'll try and remember that," Julie said.

He got up like a model about to promenade. He checked

the wave in his hair, the fold in his scarf, using the glass of the door for a mirror when he closed it behind him. Before moving away, he blew a kiss up to Mrs. Rodriguez. Juanita, when he looked down at her, offered him the handful of coins she had gathered, a gesture that made Julie sick. He took them and again flung them over the sidewalk. Across the street a flaming red sports car was waiting for him, a youthful black driver at the wheel.

Julie went out to where she could speak to Mrs. Rodriguez. "He's an elegant hunk of shit."

Mrs. Rodriguez did not understand. "Bad, bad."

"I thought maybe he was a friend of yours."

"I don't want friends like him. Gangsters. I don't like him coming here."

"I don't much want him either."

"You saw with Juanita?"

"She shouldn't be down here alone. Why isn't she in school, Mrs. Rodriguez?"

"Mind your own business."

"Okay. But don't think I'm going to look out for her."

"The street is public. You don't own the building."

"Come on, neighbor. I'm not looking for a fight. I didn't ask that guy Mack to come here. I don't want to mess with any of these cats. They're out of my class."

An expression Mrs. Rodriguez probably did not understand. "Don't you be bad to Juanita."

"Oh, hell," Julie said and went back indoors. Juanita had pretended to give each of the dolls a coin. Now she was slapping the hell out of one of them, taking back the money.

At noon Julie locked up and headed into the Eighth Avenue traffic. The street was crazy with hookers trying to pick up lunch-time quickies. There wasn't a cop in sight. Julie went on to Bourke's Electrical Shop. It felt like a kind of oasis inside.

Mr. Bourke was mending an old table lamp at the back of the shop. It looked so incongruous, that old fixture, when all around the shop were the modern appurtenances for stage and photography lighting. He glanced at her over his glasses and then back to the work in hand. His fingers were graceful and sure. They seemed to pirouette around the socket. "What can I do for you, Julie?"

"I was wondering about the girl you sent to see me, Rita."

"I wouldn't say I sent her exactly. She's always looking for someone to talk to. She picked up one of your cards from there." He indicated the Friend Julie cards alongside the cash register. "So I said why don't you go see her? She's a wise little person."

"Oh, boy."

"She hasn't been in lately. I was wondering myself."

"Maybe she has gone home," Julie said. "That's what it was all about."

"Most of them do, some time or other. But they drift back." He put the brass casing around the electrical innards and said, "There, that'll keep Mrs. Ryan out of the dark for a while."

"Is that her lamp?"

He had caught the note of surprise in Julie's voice.

"She does talk, doesn't she?"

"Some."

"It gives her something to do. Now your friend Pete I have seen. Christmas tree lights in April. 'Give me some stars, Philip Bourke,' he says." Mr. Bourke imitated Pete imitating an Irish brogue. " 'Give me an ocean of stars to fill an Irish heaven.' "

"Will you go to see the play?"

"I might since I'm a benefactor, you might say. Unless I have to stay open."

"At night?"

"Some of my best customers are moonlighters. I don't think I could stay in business without them."

"From Pete and me you couldn't make much of a living, that's for sure."

"The likes of you make the living worthwhile."

"Thanks," Julie said, suddenly shy of him. She wanted to go, but not to run.

"You're a lovely little lady, I wouldn't mind coming to you for advice myself."

"Don't!" Which he could easily misunderstand. She sputtered and laughed, trying to explain. "I mean my advice is for fun, not serious. The heavy stuff is for doctors, which is what I told Rita."

"I understand."

"I guess what I mean is I'm best with strangers, people coming in for kicks."

Mr. Bourke just looked at her while he took off his glasses and polished them with a handkerchief that was as white as snow. "I suppose Mrs. Ryan is saying I'm worse than the whores. And maybe she's right, but I don't feel that way. They're full of anger and hate and greed, and what I feel is love. It may be terrible to some people, but to me it's tender."

Julie was in agony at his frankness. Which was ridiculous. She made herself stand and be silent. Yoga or Doctor. Or herself. She was rewarded by a sudden association: "Do you know the Greek poet Cavafy, Mr. Bourke?"

"I'm not much of a reader, I'm afraid."

"I'll bring you the book if you like. He has a lot to say about love."

"My kind of love." A gentle mockery.

"Yeah."

Mr. Bourke smiled as though he was the one being tolerant. And he was. "All right."

"Maybe I'll see you at the Irish Theatre," Julie said. She was on her way when Bourke called after her and came from behind the counter.

"Stay a minute," he said, peering over his glasses at the street. "We're being observed by Mack and one of his girls. Don't look around. That's what he wants, the bastard. He'll put on a special show for us."

But Julie did look around. In time to see the pimp slap a black girl across the face and then again, this time with the back of his hand. Although Bourke called out to her not to, Julie ran to the door and shouted out at Mack, "Leave her alone, you sadistic bastard!"

It was the cowering whore who answered: "This ain't none of your business, little white cow."

Mack grinned and said, "Don't pay her no mind, sugar. She'd like some of the same thing. How about it, Sister Julie?"

"Shit," Julie said. She turned and waved at Mr. Bourke.

He beckoned her into the shop again.

When the door was closed, he said, "Don't tangle with him, Julie. He's a bad one and I'm sorry I was dumb enough not to think about him when I sent Rita to you."

"Did she tell you she'd kill herself if she didn't get out?"

"She told me."

"But you didn't believe her."

"I doubted it, but that doesn't mean she wasn't telling the truth. It only means that if I believed her, I might have felt I had to do something about it. I've got a Catholic conscience, Julie."

"A lot of stretch."

"You tell it the way it is, don't you?"

"When I can find it. Could you give me change for a quarter, Mr. Bourke?"

She intended to call Doctor Callahan, but the minute she was in the phone booth she decided against it. If Rita had been going to call Doctor, she would already have done it. The whole scene, her hand on the receiver, the dime ready, seemed like déjà vu. If only she knew what came after.

11

JULIE ARRIVED at the New Irish Theatre at a quarter to eight. Beneath her raincoat she wore white slacks and a silk paisley tunic. To cap her feeling of being well dressed, she had put on a white coral necklace Jeff had brought her from Australia. It was a warm night with the smell of the river in the air. The theater building, on West Fiftieth Street, was a former garage which in turn had been a transformed stable. The patrons were mostly people of the neighborhood with a few hard-core Irish down from the Bronx and over from Queens. They all knew one another and almost all of them, including the children, were dressed with an old-fashioned reverence for "occasion." Julie rather liked that and took off her raincoat so that it could be seen that she shared their respect. She lingered outside and watched for Pete to come to the door.

Along the street came Mrs. Ryan. Even without Fritzie she walked as though he was with her. "Well now, I was just wondering if there'd be anyone here I knew," she said when Julie went to meet her. "Most of my friends came last night for the premiere. They say it's a lovely production."

"Pete designed it."

"Ah, that's why you're here."

"I like Yeats," Julie said.

"I don't know a word he's saying, but I like the sound of it. I was wondering about you and Peter."

"There's nothing to wonder at," Julie said.

"A pity. Will I save you a seat? They're not reserved. Unless you're a VIP?"

"Save me one, I'll be in in a minute." She had the distinct feeling by then that Pete was about to stand her up again.

There was a flicker of the light over the door and the men who had smoked until the last minute disposed of their cigarettes and went in. Julie followed and spoke to the young man collecting the donations. "Is Pete Mallory backstage? I was supposed to look for him."

"I hope you find him, miss. We can't. We had to open without him last night . . . The curtain's about to go up."

Julie paid the two-dollar student rate, having to make up her mind on the spot whether to go or stay. It was one thing for Pete to stand her up, or to stand up some other person, but she did not think he was in the habit of copping out on a job. She found her way to Mrs. Ryan who had spread herself over two chairs.

"It's a lovely set," Mrs. Ryan said, moving over. There was no curtain. A country cottage, props, and bare furnishings. A small hearth glowed downstage. "You can almost smell the peat smoke. I came over when I was a child, you know, from the west of Ireland. It's the very devil to get to burn."

That of the peat, Julie assumed. If you couldn't get the peat to burn, you could certainly get burned by Pete.

The house lights went out leaving a wall of light downstage that slowly dimmed and revealed a small forest of tree trunks over which hung a dark green scrim of foliage with tiny remote lights flickering above. Pete's sea of stars in an Irish heaven.

"Will you look at that," Mrs. Ryan said and clapped her hands in delight.

They would have called the Actors Forum looking for him, Julie thought, and the Peter Mallory listed at 741 Ninth Avenue. But his work was done, actually. He had left them a show they could handle. Kiss-and-Run Pete . . .

The actors all but sang their lines and the audience to whom the words meant Ireland rocked to and fro in their seats with pleasure. Julie thought of her father whom she knew only from a handsome face in a photograph. Which made her think of *The Glass Menagerie*, from which she had once done a scene, playing Laura . . . Blow out your candles, Laura . . . She returned to *The Land of Heart's Desire:*

. . . Until she came into the land of the Faery

71

Where nobody gets old and godly and grave,
Where nobody gets old and crafty and wise,
Where nobody gets old and bitter of tongue.
And she is still there, busy with a dance
Deep in the dewy shadow of a wood,
Or where stars walk upon a mountain-top . . .

It was Yeats all right, Pete's nice noise. Damn him.

The fairy child stole the bride's soul and left the old priest helpless with the corpse of the woman. Too late, he blamed himself: "For pride comes knocking with thin knuckles on the heart." Oh, boy.

The house lights came up at the end of the curtain-raiser.

Mrs. Ryan gave a deep sigh of contentment. "I'm so glad I met you out there, Julie. I don't mind going to church alone, but I do like someone to talk to at the theater. Not that I go that often, the prices nowadays, and the things they're calling plays. Graffiti is more interesting." She gave a little pinch to her mouth, and then folded her program to point out a name to Julie. "I see Mr. Bourke has a credit for lights."

Julie was about to mention her lamp. To hell with it.

"You're very quiet," Mrs. Ryan said.

"I'm letting the play sink in."

"Is Peter here?"

"No."

"Saturday nights are the worst, aren't they? There used to be a song, Saturday night is the lonesomest night in the week."

"You bet."

"I wonder if Peter had anything to do with selecting the plays. He was the stage manager with Laura Gibson when they did street theater a few years ago. She played *Cathleen ni Houlihan* in Chelsea and the Bronx. The longshoremen coming home from the docks stopped and cheered her . . . and somebody took up a collection. Bernadette Devlin—I wonder what's happened to her."

Julie had missed the connection if there was one.

"We had such grand times in those days, such grand times."

"Did she live at the Willoughby?" Julie asked to hold up her end of the conversation. She had seen Laura Gibson in a revival of *A Streetcar Named Desire* and felt that she was pretty awful.

"Well, at the end, she did, but when I first knew her she lived at the Algonquin, no less."

Mercifully, the second play was about to start.

It seemed a variation on the same theme as the first. Julie decided she much preferred Yeats a dirty old man to the hung-up young one. Pete in the pulpit, the whore singing hymns. Goldie, Mack, Rita . . . Rita-Juanita. Julie thought she would suffocate if she did not get out soon.

After the final curtain calls, everyone was invited to stay for coffee.

"How nice," Mrs. Ryan said.

Julie proposed to escape. "I'm going on if you don't mind, Mrs. Ryan."

"I'll go with you. Let me buy you a nice glass of lager at McGowan's. It's a cheerful place on a Saturday night."

"Another time?" Julie said and put on her best smile.

"Oh, come along. You don't have to pretend with me. You've no place else you want to go or you wouldn't be here."

So they walked down Ninth Avenue, Mrs. Ryan setting the gait that had long ago been settled on her by two dogs. Julie was well aware that they would be passing Pete's building, a more persuasive circumstance than having a beer with Mrs. Ryan. She would not have gone that way alone . . . pride's thin knuckles . . . but now she was carried along by a fate there was no point in resisting.

"What was the other dog's name?" Julie asked.

"Hans. Hans and Fritz. I named them after the Katzenjammer Kids."

Who else?

It was not quite ten o'clock and yet the block in which they walked was all but deserted. Farther downtown there was considerable activity, and the few cars passing Julie and Mrs. Ryan soon slowed down to a crawl, then a halt. As the two women moved forward, traffic backed up to meet them. People crowded the sidewalk. Whatever was happening, the

police were in its midst, the prowl car light bubbles whirling.
A precinct car raced by and opened its siren. Unable to get
through, the driver mounted the sidewalk and scattered the
crowd. Julie took Mrs. Ryan's arm and hurried her. She
noted the building numbers.

"It's near Pete's. Can't you hurry, Mrs. Ryan, please?"

"Oh, my dear. Run on ahead and meet me at McGowan's."

As Julie moved into the crowd, an ambulance pulled out
and away, its siren screaming. Julie kept asking what had
happened, but no one heard or answered. Like her, everyone
else was trying to snake in closer. The police had joined
hands and forced the people back. Julie found herself surrounded by a group of weird, giggling, squealing women,
jeweled and wildly made up and trying to keep together.
Julie was jostled among them, their bodies as hard as telephone poles. Transvestites. The air now crackled with the
garble of police communication. Julie made it through to the
sawhorses in front of the building. 741.

"Stay back of the barricade, lady. This isn't a goddamn
carnival."

"I've got a friend who lives in there," Julie tried.

"Then use the telephone."

The word "murder" went through the crowd.

"Who?" Julie kept trying.

She grabbed the arm of one of the cops and hung on.
"Please listen to me!" She felt as sure as of anything in her
life that something had happened to Pete.

The officer looked round to the doorway crowded with
cops. "Russo! Talk with this girl, will you?" he shouted. He
let Julie through.

A squarish man in plain clothes intercepted her. "I'm
Detective Russo," he said.

"I just want to know . . . Pete Mallory lives here. He was
supposed to be at the theater tonight and last night and nobody knows why he didn't show up."

"We don't know the identity of the victim, miss," Russo
said. "Let's see if your friend's been checked out." He guided
her into the narrow vestibule and shone his flashlight over
the row of names on the mail panel. Certain of them were

chalked, including that of Peter Mallory. "He isn't answering his bell if he's home. Do you know anyone else in the building?"

"I don't think so." She couldn't make her eyes focus on the names.

Russo said, "Does the name Rita Morgan mean anything to you?"

The whole scene blurred. Julie caught herself just short of passing out.

12

"I'M ALL RIGHT," Julie kept saying. "I'm going to be fine in a minute." She was sitting on the steps, graffiti running crazily up and down the yellow wall alongside her. She breathed deeply of the inhalant Russo held to her nose. It brought the tears to her eyes. The detective rubbed her hands.

"Feel better now?"

"I'm okay."

"Get her into a squad car. We can talk there," another man said.

"Yes, sir." Then to Julie, to whom he offered his hand: "How are the legs?"

Julie pulled herself up. The legs trembled, but held.

With Russo and the other detective supporting her, they went out of the building. "I can walk." She got into the car which had been driven up on the sidewalk.

"A couple of questions here," the bigger of the two men said, getting in after her, "and the rest we'll get under better conditions." Russo went around the car and got in the other side. The man in charge introduced himself. "I'm Lieutenant Donleavy, Homicide. Detective Russo is a precinct officer."

"I think I know Mrs. Russo," Julie said.

"Good."

She gave her name and home address and then added, "I have . . . I guess you'd call it a business address on Forty-fourth Street."

"What kind of business, Mrs. Hayes?"

"I tell fortunes." Christ! What difference did it make?

"Well, now, aren't we in luck?" Donleavy said.

"Please . . . Tell me what happened to Pete."

76

"How do you know it's him, miss?"

"I don't. I just feel that it is. Which is crazy, except that he *is* missing."

"Do you know Rita Morgan?"

"I don't really know her. She came into my shop a couple of times. But I didn't know she lived in this building."

"Did you know she was an acquaintance of . . . Mallory, is it?"

"No."

"But he is a friend of yours?"

"Yes."

"When did you last see him?"

"It's over a week, but I talked with him on the phone—that's over a week too, but he was going to meet me at the theater tonight. He's a scene designer. When I asked for him, they said he hadn't been there for the opening last night, that they tried to find him but couldn't."

Russo took the name and address of the New Irish Theatre. Julie, remembering the program in her pocket, gave it to the detective.

"Now, miss, when did you last see Rita Morgan?"

"I think it was the same day." Julie tried to remember the sequence . . . she had seen Doctor Callahan, Rita had gone by with the cowboy and then came back alone . . . Mrs. Rodriguez and then that night the call from Pete. "It was Friday, a week ago yesterday."

"Where?"

"In my shop at the address I gave you, sir."

"Was she in the habit of patronizing your shop?" Donleavy asked.

"She wanted someone to talk to, lieutenant. In a way that's what my business is all about."

"What business is *she* in?"

Julie hesitated. To no point: they would find out. "She was on the street."

"That isn't your line, is it?"

"No, sir. No way."

"It will take us longer without your help, Mrs. Hayes," the lieutenant said, "but in the end we'll find out all there is to know about Rita. Prostitutes have a hard time keeping secrets. If your friend *is* the homicide victim, I think you'd want to tell us everything you can, now, wouldn't you?"

Julie nodded. "If."

Russo said, "Someone was the victim, and the crime did occur in her apartment."

"I have the feeling she hasn't been around for several days. I'll tell you what I can." It wasn't Rita she was trying to protect, that didn't matter now. What held her back was not knowing whether or not the girl had seen Doctor Callahan. Under no circumstances did she want to involve Doctor. "The day before yesterday a man named Mack came into my place looking for her."

"That would be her pimp," Russo said.

"Yes."

Donleavy asked, "Do you know him, Russo?"

"Yes, sir. He's the only white regular on the street. He's got an assault record, narcotics, and he's tied in with the Romano outfit."

Donleavy grunted. "Can you give us a description of the woman, Mrs. Hayes? The key things for now—something we can use with the people in the building so we can find out when she was last seen around here."

"She's about my height and build, five foot two, a hundred ten pounds. She's sixteen years old ..."

"That young?" he interrupted.

"I thought she was even younger. She looks like a child, not a bit like the others, and she wants desperately to get out of The Life and go home. That's what she came in to talk to me about."

"Where's home?"

"She wouldn't tell me. I did ask that."

"Go on with the description."

Russo took down such details as Julie gave, even to the look of innocence in the girl's smile.

Donleavy shook his head as though at the misery of it all. Julie liked him better than she had at first.

"We'll get to your friend in a minute," he said then. "I'm going to tell you how the complaint came in. The reason I'm doing this is to see if anything in it rings a bell with you. Nine-one-one got a missing persons call tonight about seven from an unidentified male caller. He gave her name and address. They tried to switch him to Missing Persons but he hung up. The first precinct men available made a routine check. The apartment door was unlocked. The officers investigated and found the victim. He had been dead for at least twenty-four hours. There was no identification on him, no wallet, no keys. Male, white, about thirty years old, slender build, height just under six feet, light brown hair that curls at the nape of his neck."

"It sounds very much like Pete," Julie said.

"All right. Put that aside for a minute. You'd be surprised how many men would fit that description. The one thing that's sure is the victim did not call the police. Who did?"

"Mack?"

"He's a strong possibility. We'll pick him up for questioning as soon as we can find him. Would you know of any connection between him and your friend?"

"No, sir."

"It seems to me," Russo said, "Mack would have been on the scene earlier than tonight. He'd have wanted her out there hustling over the weekend."

Julie remembered Mack's having said this to her: "Tell her to get her ass out on the street. I've got a big weekend coming up and I need the money." She told it now. Then: "There was a man in town with the rodeo at the Garden. She made kind of a joke of it, saying she could get him to marry her. I saw them together. Coming here, I guess. Afterwards she came back to see me; it was as though she wanted to prove to me that she really was a whore."

"Did she mention him by name?"

"No. She said he came from Laramie. She'd been with him more than once."

"Would you know him again if you saw him?"

"I think so."

"Good girl," Donleavy said. "Here's the hard one now, little lady. Do you think you could go to the morgue with Detective Russo and see if you can identify the victim?"

After a minute, Jule nodded. "Somebody has to do it."

The police radio chattered all the way downtown. Now and then the driver, to part traffic for them, used his siren.

That Julie was inside the scene instead of outsde was crazy. She didn't really know Pete at all. He had said it himself. And where was she if Pete was not . . . at the end of this mad ride? If it was not Pete Mallory? She would have involved herself unnecessarily, and God knows who else she would have involved. In time the police might have come to her about Rita. Doctor had warned her . . . There was no use looking back. No use.

Detective Russo, riding in the back seat with her, smoked silently, thoughtfully. He put the cigarette out on the floor and then threw it out the window. "Was it you that told my wife I was going to get a promotion?"

Whatever she'd expected him to ask, it wasn't that. "I didn't exactly say it. The number two kept coming up, and when I asked her if it meant anything to her, she said detective second grade. But it was me, yes, sir."

"Women are something," he said.

"She didn't come in cold, Detective Russo. Mrs. Ryan introduced us." Then: "Did you get the promotion?"

"No, but I was thinking about it just now. It used to be that I'd have been in charge of this investigation—the precinct detective answering the complaint. They've changed the system. I wasn't thinking about promotion—or maybe I was. No. What I was thinking, this is a neighborhood crime, and damn few cops in New York know that neighborhood like I do."

"And you should be back there asking questions instead of here," Julie said.

"No. This is important. But if they take me off the case after tonight, they'll be losing a good man. And I'll be losing . . . what?"

"The chance to prove it," Julie said.

"Exactly. It's like a machine they're running, like you could put all the facts into a computer. Okay. But first you got to know if they're facts. Crimes are committed by people. Maybe they don't act human, but underneath, that's what they are. This girl Rita, whatever else she is, what's more human than wanting to go home?"

"Right."

"Is that where she is now?"

"I wish I knew," Julie said.

"What I'm getting at is this: That pad of hers was as clean as a bone of personal effects. I don't think she could have cleaned out a place she'd lived in for even a few weeks if there was a guy lying there dead while she was doing it. You go in and out with trash, right? And there wasn't any trash. That had all been cleaned out ahead of time. Now either she was already gone and somebody else is the perpetrator or else this john came along at the last minute and something happened: he interrupted her plan or else he was part of the plan. Premeditated."

"How was he killed?"

"We have to wait for the medical examiner to tell us for sure. There wasn't any weapon, but it looks like a knife job."

Julie weighed the knife information. Before she had made up her mind whether or not to tell now that Rita had said she had one, Russo went on.

"There was one hell of a struggle . . ." The detective thought the better of further speculation aloud. "There's a lot of technical work to be done, and that'll tell us something."

"Like what?"

"Whether they'd had sex, for one thing."

"Yeah."

"Sorry," Russo said.

Neither of them spoke again until the car pulled up outside the Medical Examiner's office.

"This is going to be rough," Russo warned. "Have you ever seen a dead person?"

"My mother."

He took her arm.

The bleak, fluorescent lights inside the building, the murmur and soft sobs of waiting, frightened people, mostly black, who found no surcease from their own horror in the company of others whose horror might be as great. A whispery, cavernous sanctuary of violent death, of doom . . . doom . . . He's doomed, Mrs. Ryan had said of Pete. How could she have known?

Russo checked in with a medical examiner who immediately dialed an inside phone number. Julie picked up the words *autopsy room*.

"They haven't taken him in yet," the gray man said, hanging up the phone. He took off his sports jacket and put on a dirty white coat, and then led the way through a corridor to a heavy steel door.

Russo held onto Julie's arm with hard fingers. "Breathe through your mouth," he said, "and remember death stinks. Let me go down ahead of you."

The sickly sweet odor came up like a rotten blanket into her face. She clung to the railing going down the narrow, curved stairwell. From the moment she started down, she kept her eyes on Detective Russo's back; she saw on the periphery of her vision, nonetheless, the wall of drawers and the sacked forms on wheeled tables. She thought of Jeff who often spoke of walking among the dead, the battlefield dead, the flood dead, the living dead, the dead living. Which was how she felt. And flies. Where had flies come from so early in April? Or were they always here waiting new carrion? She kept thinking of Jeff, his fastidious nose wrinkled in distaste at some social gaucherie, and his hard straightnosed probe into work that had to be done no matter how difficult. Somebody had to do it—when she had said that, she was quoting Jeff. No matter what or where his assignment, he always said, Somebody has to do it, and set about packing his bags.

They waited, the examiner ordering by number the corpse he wanted delivered. Her eyes met Russo's large, dark Italian eyes, liquid with sympathy and then, at the wavering of hers, growing tough and fixed, as though to keep her on her feet. The attendant grinned at her and, on his way, moved as though he relished his job, a jaunty, devil-may-care stride. He even slapped, as he might a girl's ass, a bagged corpse as he passed it. Her hatred for him stiffened her, helped her endure. He wheeled in the sheeted figure and maneuvered the trolley with the flair of a car-park jockey. He flashed her a smile again.

"Goddamn you." She must have said it aloud, for Detective Russo squeezed her arm.

"That's the girl," he said. "You're all right?"

"You bet."

The medical examiner took hold of the covering with heavy, thick fingers and after the briefest hesitation lifted it away from the face of the victim.

It was Pete. Gray as putty, the eyes closed, the mouth still open as though he had been about to speak when he no longer could. But unmistakably Pete.

Julie nodded and put her hand to where his arm might be underneath the coarse sheet. There was an awful softness where she had expected stone. Detective Russo turned her away and guided her to the steps. They climbed up and up a staircase, it seemed, without an end. Then at last the door. A way out.

Russo gave her a chair in an anteroom to the main office and brought her water in a paper cup. She shook her head. She could still smell death. She was afraid she'd be sick if she took the water, for the smell was also a taste.

Russo drank the water himself and threw the cup into a wastebasket. He sat at the desk with his notebook open. "His full name, Mrs. Hayes?"

She spelled the last name.

"Do you know his next of kin?"

"No, sir."

"Any relatives in New York that you know of?"

"I don't think there are any, but I don't really know."

Russo phoned her identification to the precinct desk where it was to be relayed at once to Donleavy.

By the time they got out to the waiting car, Donleavy had radioed instructions that Russo was to get Mrs. Hayes's complete statement and have it transcribed and signed before going off duty.

All Julie could think of was the guy at the morgue trundling Pete around like a side of beef. Except that it wasn't Pete anymore. It wouldn't matter much to Pete what they did with the remains. To whom would it matter . . . besides herself?

Russo tape-recorded her statement, playing phrases back when she asked so that she could qualify or elaborate. "Just tell it in your own way," he had asked, "everything about the girl you can remember, about the pimp, the cowboy, anything that comes to mind. Then we'll go over it again and see what else we can squeeze out. Okay?"

Just like Doctor, except for the squeeze part. She was trying hard to convince herself that Rita would not have called Doctor Callahan. But if she had called her, it was Doctor's business to decide whether or not the police should know about it. Once Julie had clarified that issue in her own mind, she was better able to deal with Russo's questions. And somewhere along in the interrogation, she became aware of the human being trying to coax out of her his next assignment, as it were. A lot was riding for him on poor Pete's death. Russo couldn't be much over thirty, dark complexioned, very Italian looking, a neighborhood kid who grew up to be a cop, and then one step more, a detective. She felt caring of him, almost maternal, and much older. It was a good feeling in the midst of so much that was strange and bad.

Julie waited a long time in the cubicle of a room with its single window protected by wire mesh. Then, because no one had said she had to stay there, she wandered in the hall, stepping aside for patrolmen and their prisoners on the way to the briefing room or detention cells, whores and derelicts, sullen captives . . . She looked into the briefing room in passing, the walls hung with wanted flyers, the long table crowded with cops and perpetrators, one to one in their paired concern with the offense that had brought them together. Julie found herself wishing she could go in and look into the face of each one of them and ask the question, Why?

A wall clock showed one-thirty.

She went back to where Russo had left her and waited. He had promised to take or send her home in a police car after she read and signed her transcribed statement. When he returned with it, he brought along a carton of coffee for her. She read carefully, noticing that everything was left in, qualifications, corrections following that which she had corrected, even to Rita's mention of her kid brother. She felt she had been thorough. Russo had been even more so.

Just as she was signing, Donleavy came into the little room and crowded it with his presence. He waited until she was finished and then said, "Take a walk through the briefing room with Detective Russo, Mrs. Hayes. See if there's anyone in there you recognize."

There were more black faces than white and only a sentimental fool would say what their expressions meant. The only why that concerned most of them was why they had been caught. They came to a middle-aged man, well-dressed, his arms folded; his face was yellowish, like a faded suntan, and the mark of a hat band came just beneath his hairline. After a brief glimpse at Julie, he stared with bloodshot eyes at the uniformed cop opposite him. Unlike the other officers at the table, this one had no notebook before him. He was sitting in, a dummy. Julie hardly knew whether she recognized the cowboy or deduced who he was. He was third from the end.

"I wouldn't want to say positively," Julie qualified when they returned to where Donleavy was waiting in the corridor.

"Not necessary," Donleavy said. "A psychological test on the gent, you might say. Thank you very much, Mrs. Hayes."

13

SHE AWOKE STRUGGLING out of a horrible, disgusting dream. In it she was about to have her picture taken, hundreds of people around, and she had turned for a quick look into a mirror. But it was not her face that she saw, it was the oval of her backside as though she were bent over, and in its center was a glowering, rheumy eye.

The phone rang. What had awakened her was the clicking sound that sometimes preceded the ring. Just as she picked up the receiver she remembered what had happened the night before.

"Julie, it's Amy Ross. Did I waken you?"

"What time is it?"

"It's eleven. Something terrible happened to Pete Mallory. He's dead."

"I know."

"I just heard it on the radio. Everybody was looking for him Friday and he must've been dead then."

"Yeah."

"When did you find out?"

"I identified his body at the morgue last night." Pete's mouth had looked like an eye.

"My God . . . Julie, are you alone? I live on Tenth Street. Shall I come over?"

"Thanks."

She put the receiver back on the hook and pushed the phone farther away from her, to the very edge of the bed-side table. Her clothes were strewn where she had dropped them on Jeff's bed. For hours she had lain, going over and over Detective Russo's interrogation and her answers. And the smell of the morgue had persisted. Then finally sleep and dreams of which she could only remember the anxiety. She drew her arm back under the covers and pulled her knees up into the fetal position. When she had seen her mother dead, she had felt she was looking at a stranger. She hadn't wanted to touch her as she had Pete. Jeff had kept trying to console her when she didn't feel the need to be consoled at all. Then, because she was ashamed, she had pretended. Like sex when she didn't want it. Thinking now of the putrid, all-pervasive smell of which Pete was part, and the impulse to touch, to save, to understand, to what?—thinking of it now, she was filled with sexual urgency.

Amy Ross brought bagels and cream cheese. And she brought something of the outdoors into a house that had felt sealed up. She wasn't even a friend, but she became one on the spot, giving orders, taking over.

"You look like hell. Why don't you take a shower? I'll find the coffee and fix breakfast."

Amy had picked up the Sunday *Times* marked "Hayes" in the vestibule. Sunday: at St. Malachy's they'd have to send in the understudy. Julie felt a little more like herself. The bath helped even more. But not once, even while brushing her hair, did she glance in the mirror.

The table was set, a split bagel in the toaster, the coffee ready. Amy came from the parlor where she had been exploring. "This apartment's something. I don't know what I expected."

"After Julie's Place?" Julie's Place: it did exist. She reached for the coffee.

"You're married to Geoffrey Hayes, aren't you?"

"Sometimes."

"My father's always quoting him."

"That's about right," Julie said.

"You'll feel better when you have something to eat." Amy pushed down the spring in the toaster. When the bagel popped up, she spread a half with cream cheese for Julie.

Julie ate without tasting, numb and silent. Amy ate a bite or two of the other half, pushed it away, and then picked it up and finished it. Then she ate a tiny bite of cream cheese from the knife. She was fighting weight, getting a little plump in the waist. Julie began to think about her. She had seen her in the production of *Streetcar,* in which Laura Gibson had starred.

"I saw you play Stella," she said. "You were good." Was she? It had to be said anyway.

"Thank you. Pete designed that production, you know."

"I'd forgotten."

"You shouldn't. That was the best part. He used film as counterpoint. Remember? I wanted terribly to do Blanche DuBois. I don't mean Laura Gibson wasn't good. Well, she wasn't, but that wasn't her fault. People said she was too old for the part, but it wasn't that; she was already ill."

"What about her and Pete? Was there something?"

"Oh, yes, there was something."

"Was he in love with her?"

Amy shrugged. "I don't know about Pete. Were you in love with him?"

"On my way to it maybe. I don't know. It's all mixed up now."

"There was something tremendous between him and Laura. Personally, I don't think it was bed. But she wasn't the mother type either."

"Was Pete homosexual?"

"The gay boys adore him."

"So?"

"So I don't know. I'm just saying."

"What did they say on the radio," Julie asked, "about what happened last night?"

"A member of the Actors Forum—they had to get that in naturally—found slain in another apartment of the building where he lived. The police are searching for the apartment's occupant. I forget her name, I'd never heard it before."

"Rita Morgan."

"An older woman, I'll bet anything," Amy said.

"Sixteen. A prostitute."

"What?" Amy made a face of disbelief.

"Screwy, isn't it?"

Amy said, "I mean if Pete wanted sex, I know a dozen kids . . ."

"Yeah."

"Including me, if you want to know the truth. I kind of

like the borderline kooks. But like I told you at the Forum that night, Kiss-and-Run Pete. Julie, a prostitute in this day and age? It doesn't make sense."

"There's a lot of them on the street."

"But they're out for a different breed of cat. I don't even think Pete could afford the going rate."

"The coming rate," Julie said in that reflexive pattern. But it put her in mind of a play Pete had made on the same word, "Nobody comes natural anymore."

"Amy?"

"Yes?"

"They found his body in her apartment, but it doesn't necessarily mean he'd been to bed with her. The police don't know that. He could have known her like I did—somebody she could tell her troubles to." She told Amy of Rita's coming into the shop.

"That sounds more like it," Amy said of Pete's relationship with the girl.

"What's Pete's background, do you know?"

"Midwest, a town outside Chicago. I think he has a sister living out there. I know he went to Yale on some kind of fellowship. He was a protégé of Ira Windsor . . ."

"The designer," Julie said.

"Now that relationship . . . everybody took for granted, you know? Windsor's the queen of queens. It's too bad Laura Gibson isn't alive. She knew Pete like nobody else did."

"It's too bad Pete isn't alive," Julie said and poured herself another cup of coffee.

"You should have seen her when they were doing street theater. *Cathleen ni Houlihan*. I mean the play is nothing today, but she was . . . a presence. Something went wrong for her to have missed being a star. She drank a lot. Maybe it was that. But my God, think of the drunks who made it."

"I saw *Cathleen ni Houlihan* last night. Just last night. It seems like years. I was supposed to meet Pete there. Afterwards a friend and I walked down Ninth Avenue. There was a crowd and the police and I wanted to know. Boy, did I find out."

"Pete wasn't ever going to make it big either," Amy said,

following her own train of thought. "It has to do with being at the right place at the right time."

"Pete avoided the right places."

"You can't go back to doing small parts after you've played leads—unless at some place like the Forum. Even there." Amy had lapsed entirely into thoughts of herself and her own career. That was the thing about actors. Every time you told them about somebody else, they told you about themselves.

"I wonder what happens next," Julie said. She thought of Mrs. Ryan. How long had she waited at McGowan's Tavern? Wherever she was right now, she'd certainly be talking about Pete Mallory. *Peter* Mallory. And her friend Laura Gibson. "What's the latest disaster at the Willoughby?" Mr. Bourke . . . who was somehow the link among them all . . . Could Rita have gone home to *Pete's* home town? She'd refused to tell Julie where home was. Why? What difference could she have thought it would make to Julie? Could it mean that Rita knew she and Pete were friends?

"Amy, how old was Pete?"

"Thirty-one or two."

"Did he go home summers . . . or on vacation?"

"You mean to Illinois? I don't think so. I don't really know. I'm not even sure about the sister now. It was something at the back of my mind."

"Did you know he'd studied for the priesthood?"

"I knew he was a Catholic. I mean a real one, practicing. So was Laura Gibson."

The name kept coming up. "Why do you keep mentioning her, Amy? I don't mean you shouldn't. I'm just asking—do you think of her automatically every time you think of Pete?"

"No . . . Well, it's funny. I almost do. You see Pete was a strange cat. Every time you'd think you were getting to know him, that he liked you, that you were getting underneath that offhand way of his, he'd walk away. It was like a comedy routine, something in an old-time movie where the hero goes into the burning building, rescues the girl, and carries her out in his arms, then drops her on the sidewalk and walks away. But he wasn't like that with Laura. He'd be waiting for her after theater, he even helped her take off her makeup. It was—oh, hell, it was touching, and I know that when she was dying and didn't have any money, Pete paid her bills."

"Where'd he get the money?"

Amy shrugged. "Don't know."

"When did he come to New York, how long ago?"

Amy thought about it. "I still have the *Streetcar* program, and I think his bio gives the date he was at Yale. I'll call you when I get home."

Without thinking of what she was doing, Julie got up and cleared the dishes.

"I'll go," Amy said. "I can take a hint."

"I'm sorry. I was thinking. I am grateful to you, Amy. I needed help this morning and you were it." She thought of Doctor, who had at no time been very far out of mind, only too distressing a presence to be allowed all the way in.

"What would you say to my organizing a memorial for Pete at the Forum?"

"Great." Julie could think of nothing that seemed less relevant just then. Except that any number of people might have things to say about Pete that she would have no other way of finding out.

"I'll think about it. Not everyone was as fond of Pete as you and I."

"Let's make it an open invitation anyway," Julie said, and then, catching a little gleam of resentment in Amys eye, "I'll help out in any way I can, but you're the preacher."

At the door, Amy said, "I hope you don't mind my saying this, I just realized what Pete saw in you. You've got an unusual way of saying things, way out, and yet they're right. Pete was like that. He did things that worked by contrast, not just illustration." Then, thinking over what she had said, she added, "I must remember that for the memorial."

"Write it down," Julie said.

She was bolting the door after Amy's departure when the phone rang. A midtown precinct officer identified himself. Detective Russo would be grateful if she would accompany him to Broome Street and assist the police artist who was preparing a sketch of the missing witness, Rita Morgan. Julie agreed to be ready at two-thirty.

Amy called within the hour and read her Pete's biography from the program of *A Streetcar Named Desire:*

" 'Peter Mallory (designer) met Laura Gibson while he was studying at The Yale Drama School on the Ira Windsor Fellowship in 1967. He has worked with her in every play in which she has appeared since, including the off-Broadway revivals of *Juno and the Paycock, Red Roses for Me, Medea,* and *The Chalk Garden.* He designed, mounted, and stage managed last year's highly successful New York Street Festival Theater. A native of Libertytown, Illinois, Mr. Mallory studied drawing at the Chicago Art Institute and design at the Goodman Theater in Chicago. He is considered one of the most promising young innovators in multimedia design.' "

"That's it," Amy said. "We opened January 17 and closed in April. Laura Gibson died last fall."

"Thanks," Julie said. "You're great."

Julie could not figure out why the production had made so little impression on her, or more to the point, such a bad one apparently that she had not thought of Pete these past couple of weeks in connection with it. Then she had it: Jeff had despised it. It represented everything wrong with American theater, an assault upon the senses, a psychedelic trip, self-indulgent, a travesty on artistic discipline, et cetera, et cetera. A snow job. After which she had looked for a new hiding place herself, taking courses toward becoming a psychiatric social worker. It turned out that Jeff had even stronger opinions in that area. And when she again crawled out from under the snow, Jeff had suggested Doctor Callahan. For Julie.

14

DETECTIVE RUSSO'S SOULFUL EYES were puffy and blood-shot, but he grinned at Julie, leaned across the seat, and opened the door for her. "It's me," he said. "I'm still on the job."

"Great," Julie said. The car reeked of shaving lotion.

"My wife sends her regards."

"Thanks."

His eyes rested on her a moment as he looked around be-fore pulling out ahead of the oncoming cars. The motor sputtered and then decided to keep going. "It's my own car," he said. "I don't drive it much."

A poor thing, but his own. "It's stiff," Julie said.

"I should have asked you last night if you needed a sleep-ing pill," Russo said, apparently measuring her sleep by the length of her sentences. "Do you live alone?"

"Most of the time. My husband's a newspaperman."

"No kidding."

"I'd as soon keep his name out of this, however."

"I understand. It's nobody's business, including mine. But I knew you weren't just anybody."

"But I am," Julie said. "It's Jeff who's special."

"That's who's special in our house too, me. You know, my wife owned a beauty shop when I married her. She gave it up when I got made a detective because she thought it might hurt my image."

Or hers as a detective's wife, Julie wondered. "She's very ambitious for you."

"Yeah. Maybe if we had kids . . ."

The cure-all, kids. "They grow up," Julie said.

"Oh, man. We got a sergeant in the department. He's got

five kids, from junior high up. Two of them already busted for drugs. 'Those beautiful babies,' he keeps saying. 'What happened to them?' "

Julie thought of Rita. "What will you do with the picture if it turns out to look like Rita?"

"Don't worry, it'll turn out like her. This guy's a whiz, but we won't use it till you say okay. You and the cowboy, Matt Arlen. We'll get back to him with it before he takes off for Wyoming. We'll sweep the neighborhood with it, give it to the newspapers, and then see what happens. You never saw a street as clean as Eighth Avenue this morning. There isn't a hustler in sight. That's how it'll be for a couple of days. Then one by one, they'll crawl out of their holes."

"Except Rita."

"That depends. She could still be here—at some other address. If it turns out she's clean, she'll come out as soon as she knows we're looking for her. The cowboy saw her Wednesday night so we know she was here then. He'd signed her up for every night in the week through Saturday, and the poor dumb bastard gave her a hundred dollars in advance. She said she wanted to buy a present for her kid brother's birthday."

"F.A.O. Schwarz," Julie said.

"What?"

"She used to go there and look at the toys when she got homesick."

"No kidding." Russo pulled to the side of the street and wrote himself a note. "That wasn't in your statement, was it?"

"I guess not."

"You can never tell," Russo said. "Maybe she really did want to buy a present for her brother."

"I'd have believed her."

"Most prostitutes are pretty convincing liars, Julie. Okay to call you Julie?"

"Everybody does."

"I'm Dom as in Dominic. I'm playing with the idea that once she got the hundred bucks extra in hand, she cleared out on the cowboy. Thursday, Friday, and Saturday, three nights at twenty-five bucks a trick, she was still twenty-five

94

ahead and without having to come across."

Women's lib, Julie screamed silently.

"Tricks on tricks," Russo said, pleased with himself. "This is only one cop's theory, of course. It may not hold up."

"If it does hold up, it means somebody else killed Pete."

"That's the way I was going. Women don't generally use knives, except in a family situation."

"Did I say in my statement she told me she had a knife? God, I'm so foggy."

"You did say it. It would have been some oversight if you forgot that."

"But I didn't really believe she had a knife."

"You said that too, and for the time being, I go along with it. Me, alone. Donleavy says, get her, grill her. That's your job. He likes to keep the heavy stuff for himself. Which is okay by me."

"What you said about family—I've been trying to figure out if she and Pete could have come from the same place in Illinois. There has to be some connection."

"Not if her name is Rita Morgan, which it probably isn't."

"How do you know?"

"Well, now . . ." He broke into his own train of thought to ask: "Did you know Mallory had a sister?"

"I found it out this morning. He came from a town called Libertytown, Illinois."

"That's the place. Donleavy decided last night that since I was such a good neighbor type, I ought to be the one to call her. We'd got an order and entered Mallory's apartment by then. We found out he called his sister at seven-forty Thursday night. That was his last known contact. He was supposed to get back to the Irish Theatre for a dress rehearsal by eight o'clock, but they went on without him. Nobody from there tried to get in touch with him till the next day. So sometime between seven-forty and midnight—probably between then and eight o'clock—he went down one flight of stairs to the apartment right under his, and that was it. Want to hear the details?"

"You bet." Julie clinched her teeth.

"He was lying face down on the bed, a wound in the chest and two more in the back. It was one of the back wounds that was fatal. The weapon was a knife with a narrow, six-inch blade, a wide hilt. There was a lot of blood." He glanced at Julie. "Are you all right?"

"Keep going."

"He was wearing slacks and a tee shirt, no underwear. There was no linen on the bed, just a blanket, pad, and spread, so if they had sex, it probably wasn't premeditated. The pathology report isn't in yet." He paused.

"I get it," Julie said.

"He didn't have a key on him. In fact, the only thing in his pocket was a stub of a pencil. We figured at first he'd been rolled—no wallet on him. We found that upstairs afterwards, but still no key, and he had locked his door before going down. Somebody must've taken the key with them. There's no sign of them having gone near his place, but we can't say that for sure."

"What about shoes?"

"Smart girl. One on, one off. It came off with the lace still tied."

"So he probably didn't take it off himself."

"Right." Russo drew the car up to the curb alongside a fire hydrant and cut the motor. "Let's just sit for a minute, and you tell me how it looks to you."

"It doesn't look like Rita. I'll tell you that. Her place wasn't locked, right?"

Russo nodded.

"When she was all set to split, could she have given the key to Pete, maybe to give to somebody? Maybe she was going to sublet. How about that? He went down to show the apartment for her . . ."

Russo was shaking his head. "Her pimp paid the rent, Julie. He put her in there and paid the bills."

"All right. Let's say Pete and Rita were friends, just friends. Let's say she told him the same things she told me about wanting to go home, et cetera . . ." Julie paused. "I've just remembered: I told Pete on the phone about her coming to see me, and he never let on that he knew her."

"It's not exactly the kind of friendship a man boasts about to a respectable young lady," Russo suggested.

"I guess," Julie said, but she was pretty sure that whatever

96

had kept Pete from mentioning it had nothing to do with her respectability. "He did ask me if she'd told me where home was . . ."

"I'm going to make a note of that," the detective said, and did.

"Then he kidded me about not being able to give her the fare home, something like that. One thing I feel sure about, Pete would have encouraged her." Even as she said it, Julie wasn't all that sure. She had done a lot of fantasizing about Pete that had more to do with herself than with him. He was a pretty cynical guy.

Russo said, "Who'd have wanted to stop her?"

"Mack, of course. A rough character."

"And a petty operator," Russo added.

"Hey, if he'd been knocking her around, Pete wouldn't have just stood by. I am sure of that."

"The gallant type?"

"All right," Julie said defensively.

"Could be that," Russo said. "And while they skirmished she took off. In which case, let me ask you this: Do you think she'll come back and give testimony against the pimp?"

"She'd almost have to, wouldn't she?"

"Voluntarily or otherwise, yes."

"Then she isn't ever going to get home. Unless she's already there."

"It'll be a short visit."

He put the car into motion again. Presently he said, "His sister was coming out here next week to see this play he was working on. It was rotten, having to tell her what happened to him. On the phone yet. Seems like we could've waited and had the local cops break it to her. But, Donleavy's the boss . . . and of course we wouldn't 've known about the phone call till later. I did ask her if she knew anybody by the name of Rita Morgan. I also checked the phone company for the name Morgan in Libertytown and environs. Seems like a common name, but not out there apparently."

"What's the sister like? Could you tell?"

"I couldn't tell. It was after midnight. I'd woken her up. I did most of the talking. I asked her if there was anyone else in the house or a neighbor she could call to be with her.

Name is Helen Mallory so she isn't married. I got the idea she was a schoolteacher or librarian, you know."

"I know."

"It gave me a funny feeling, thinking how she'd be finding her way to the phone through one of these small-town houses you see in the movies, turning on lights as she went along. And there I was on the other end of the phone, sitting at her brother's desk with a swarm of technicians around me, cracking jokes, doing their job like it was all in a night's work. Which it is."

"I wish I could see Pete's apartment," Julie said.

"Ask his sister. We got it sealed up for now, but she's the one who's got the say about what to do with her brother's effects. Do you know anybody by the name of Laura?"

"Laura Gibson, an actress."

"I figured that. Her picture's on his desk."

"She's dead too."

Russo nodded and swore softly at someone who cut in ahead of him. "He's got an interesting photograph collection. Know anything about that?"

"Stage design?"

"Not exactly." He looked at her and then back to the street. "Stills from a porn movie."

"My God," Julie said, and then, almost to herself, "I didn't really know Pete at all." She sighed deeply, needing the breath, and wondered whether she was more surprised at Pete or at herself for being all that surprised. "Hey, I wonder if there'd be a picture of Rita."

"I was wondering that too."

"So? Where are they?"

Russo took one hand from the wheel and rubbed the back of his neck. "He wasn't exactly interested in physiognomies."

Julie's impulse to laugh was cut short. Suddenly she remembered her dream. Physiognomies.

Russo said: "I've got a few of them in an envelope back there." He indicated the back seat.

"Shall I look at them now?"

"They'll have a magnifying glass at the studio."

Julie was quite willing to wait. She thought about Pete's sister to whom the pictures, whatever their content, whatever they told her about Pete, would now belong. Did she, like Pete, go to church every Sunday, and did she sometimes pray, like Mrs. Rodriguez, to the open heart of Jesus? Russo was probably a Catholic too. For somebody who wanted no part of the scene, she'd sure as hell plunked herself down center stage.

In the dingy loft studio, Detective Russo introduced her to Sergeant Greenberg who, pleasant enough to Julie, took out his complaint on Russo of having to come in on Sunday and instead of getting time and a half was going to have to take a day off mid-week.

"You're going to love your work today," Russo said, opening his briefcase. "Dirty pictures. These are the ones with faces. Set 'em up so Mrs. Hayes can look at them."

"You mean mask them?" Greenberg said with a half-snicker as he turned the eight-by-ten prints around and around to satisfy his own curiosity, viewing them from all angles.

"You know what we want," Russo said tersely. His face had taken on a ruddy glow.

Julie, to clear the air, picked up a photograph, chosen at random, and looked at it. It shocked hell out of her: half a man's torso, the enormous penis erect, with two nude women, one on either side, facing the camera, lying on their bellies and both about to touch the center piece. The photo had been shot at a slight angle. "The leaning tower of Pisa," she said. It broke the cops up. "Neither of the girls is Rita Morgan."

They were able to proceed with something approaching laboratory conditions. Greenberg provided a magnifying glass and turned on more light. Rita was not in the collection.

Greenberg brought out an album of pictures of women, some photos, some clipped from magazines. Julie studied them under his direction, looking for eyes, expression, hairline, any individual feature that looked at all like the missing girl.

Russo had two other descriptions of Rita besides Julie's, the building superintendent's at 741 and the cowboy's. The latter tallied with Julie's very closely, even to the "kind of innocent smile."

"Give me a couple of hours," Greenberg said. "Go see a porn movie."

Funny.

Outdoors, Russo proposed to Julie that they go over to Chinatown and have something to eat. She did not expect to have much appetite, but it was something to do. "Are you on the case permanently now?"

"Nobody's on any case permanently, not nowadays. But I've been temporarily detached to work with Homicide."

Temporarily detached. Julie hoped that her present feeling of detachment was temporary. She had only just begun to feel involved with her life when this had happened. Nothing that was coming out about Pete related to the guy she thought she knew. "Who knows anybody?" she said aloud.

"I see what you mean. There's times I don't even know myself. No kidding, sometimes at night, or mornings, when I get home and take off my thirty-eight"—he patted the gun holstered under his arm—"and lock it away the bureau drawer, I'll look at myself in the mirror and say, Now, who are you, Russo?"

"There ought to be a pretty good answer to that."

"Thank you."

"Well?"

He smiled and cocked his head thoughtfully, the ignition key in his hand where it rested on the steering wheel. "Dominic Russo, second-generation American whose grandfather peddled fish from the back of a Ford truck and put his four sons into the wholesale fish business and local politics. I could have gone in a lot of directions. A lot of what they say is crap, but I do have a godfather."

"Godfather with a capital *G?*"

"He thinks it's pretty capital, and it probably is. Yeah." He was about to turn the key in the ignition. "You know, we could walk from here."

"Then let's. I'd rather walk any day. I'll bet I've walked every foot of Manhattan. I ought to be a cop."

"They don't walk much, especially the lady cops. It's too dangerous."

"They ought to dress like me," Julie said. "I really go around in plain clothes."

"You're a kook," Russo said, grinning.

Sergeant Greenberg came up with a good likeness of Rita except for one thing: "She's not that old," Julie said.

"Maybe she will be by the time Russo finds her," he said grumpily. Then: "Let's clean it up a little and see what happens."

It was remarkable to see the change he wrought with a few erasure rubs.

"That's it," Julie said. "Gosh."

"Funny. I'd have thought it was closer the first time," Greenberg said. He put the sketch in an envelope and gave it to Russo. He left the building with them.

Russo proposed to show the drawing to the cowboy before sending it to photography. It was the pretext on which the police had delayed his leaving the city.

In the car Julie said, "Now what?"

"There ought to be other stuff in the hopper by now. A half-dozen detectives have been on the case since morning. Sift, check out, pray, and needle the lab people."

Julie was tempted to ride uptown with him to Forty-fourth Street.

Russo didn't like the idea of her going back there right away. "Do you have a phone in the place?"

"No."

"First thing in the morning, get one installed. Have the phone company call me at Midtown if you have to."

"I wasn't thinking of that permanent an establishment when I started."

"That's even better. Stay away from there."

"I'll call the phone company," Julie said.

"That's what I figured you'd do." Russo drove in silence for a time, spinning off his own associations. "I'd give a lot to know who put in that missing persons squeal. The cowboy swears he didn't do it, and that makes sense. When a hooker stands a guy up, he generally takes for granted she's been busted and stays clear."

"Where was he going to meet her?"

"She was to come to his motel room."

"But when I saw them, they were going to her place. At

least, I think that's where they were going."

"They were. She was the one who changed the locale. Starting Wednesday night, eleven-thirty, which was when she collected the hundred bucks."

"It seems to me he'd have wanted to check her place when she didn't show up the next night. You know, to see if there'd been a mixup."

"I'd also like to know if she was on the street Wednesday night before their date. One trick a night isn't exactly hustling."

Julie thought Mr. Bourke might know, but she decided against volunteering him. "Mack would know." Him she didn't mind volunteering.

"If you see him, Julie, stay clear, but let me know. We want him."

"You bet."

The phone calls began to come in soon after she got back to Seventeenth Street: people she hardly knew at the Forum and friends of Jeff's . . . and hers, she supposed, although there were not many friends of Jeff's whom she considered her friends.

Anne Briscoe's call was typical: "Darling, what have you been up to? You *are* the same Julie Hayes . . ."

I'm Janet, she wanted to say, remembering the last time she had spoken to Anne Briscoe to get out of her dinner party.

Somewhere back there long ago, she had been living a sort of life, shipping between two seas, having her thrice-weekly sessions with Doctor Callahan and writing letters of reassurance to Jeff that she was fine, that everything was fine. She decided not to answer the phone anymore that night and then changed her mind to take one more call.

"This is Doctor Callahan. I'm sorry about your friend Peter Mallory." The tone was as brusque as ever.

"Thanks."

"I think it would be a good thing for you to keep your regular Monday appointment."

"Me too."

"I have made the hour available."

"Thank you . . . Doctor?"

"Yes."

"Did Rita call you?"

Silence.

"I'm not going to tell anyone."

"I saw her," Doctor said and hung up.

15

Doctor Callahan showed neither welcome nor sympathy. She did take one clean, direct look at Julie at the door. Eye to eye. Then she thumped into her office, leaving Julie to close the door between office and vestibule as always. With a sweeping gesture, she directed Julie onto the couch.

"Right away?"

"Yes."

Doctor settled in her chair and released the brake. A power break . . . the arrogance of power . . .

" 'Pride comes knocking with thin knuckles on the heart,' " Julie said, prone.

"What?"

"It's a line from a play I just thought of."

Silence.

"Pride, police, passion. Passion. I thought I didn't have any. That's crap. I know I do, but I can't get it out. I can't bleed. Like a thorn is stuck in me, the sacred heart of Jesus, Pete in church reading during the Mass, a half-assed priest, a prostitute can sing hymns—'Holy God, we praise thy name.' Her bouncing ass, my dream, my face turned into my backside with one eye bleeding at me. Pete's mouth in the morgue like an eye and no eyes, and his arm like jelly under the sheet. I masturbated in bed the next morning. I thought of him, the way he was dead, and I never knew him. I never knew any man. My father using the church to get away, free, home safe in Ireland. Are there any whores in Ireland? Who needs whores if everybody plays? Street games, Pete called it, and everybody plays, the woman upstairs with her stunted child, Little Orphan Annie, empty eyes. She tears her dolls apart and loves them till she hates them. She picked up the pimp's

104

money and gave it back to the bastard so he could throw it down like seed on the dead ground. Whore seed. Magdalene's daughter."

Dead. Blank. Nothing.

"What about Magdalene's daughter?"

"I made it up. I wrote it in my notebook the first day on Forty-fourth Street."

"Who is Magdalene?"

"Mary Magdalene in the Bible."

"Who was her daughter?"

"I just made it up. It sounded good, like the title for a book."

"You're writing a book?"

"Something. I always am, and then I don't ever finish."

"Why?"

"I'm afraid."

"Of what?"

"Failure."

"What's failure?"

"Not being able to say what I want to say."

"What do you want to say?"

"Something about me. Something that's real, deep, true. Sure, beautiful. I thought Pete was beautiful. When he said, 'They don't know a ceiling light from the star of Bethlehem.' That's beautiful to be able to say that. 'Give me an ocean of stars for an Irish heaven.' He studied to be a priest. Hey! now I know what was wrong in church when I saw him. It wasn't obscene, him doing his thing on stage. I was jealous! And ashamed though I didn't know it. I felt lousy, seeing him behind the altar railing. I wished I hadn't seen him."

"It spoiled your fantasy, perhaps."

"Maybe, except I didn't know I was doing much of that then. He'd stood me up the night before. Just didn't show up, but sent me a lovely note. I can say it by memory. 'Friend Julie, I'm sorry to have gone into my vanishing act. A sick friend needed me and since that doesn't happen very often I stood by. May the gods inspire you and the fates send custom.' "

She waited for Doctor's comment. Nothing.

"That's all," she said.

"Who was the sick friend?"

"I don't know. I never really thought about it then. Now . . ."

"*Then:* stay with then. You didn't think it might be a woman?"

"You mean Rita?"

"I'm talking about you. Did *you* think it might be a woman he was with?"

"No."

"And yet you were jealous of him in the church."

"Crazy. No, it isn't. Everybody at the Forum thinks Pete was homosexual. I don't think so."

"But you didn't think this sick friend excuse might be another woman."

"You sound like a Victorian spinster!"

"Why are you angry?"

"Because that's what *I* am. A Victorian spinster. I'm an oddball, an anachronism. I don't even love my husband and I'm as faithful as a seeing-eye dog."

"So you fantasize a homosexual."

"Oh, shit."

"That's probably what it is, shit."

"You don't let up, do you, Doctor?"

"Are you in mourning?"

"What does that mean?"

"Do you feel pain or do you pretend?"

"I don't pretend. I'm not going to pretend anything anymore. When my mother died, I pretended all over the place. And I didn't feel a goddamn thing. I don't know what I feel about Pete. Why did I masturbate? I was lying there doubled up thinking of him. What is it? Necro . . . necro-something. The whole feeling of rottenness, dead, decaying . . . But why did I feel that way? I wanted to go back, back, deep back . . . that look at myself, my behind with an eye, what looked like an eye staring back at me from the mirror, one, homo . . . I don't know! Death, birth, one eye, Father, one church, immaculate conception, one, one . . . But I'm two! Jeff wants me to come to Paris for a month in June if you say it's all right."

"What do you say?"

"He didn't ask me what I say."

"What *do* you say?"

"The honeymoon part turns me off, a second honeymoon. I never thought I'd get through the first. He should've taken my mother. The way she flirted with him. I was ashamed for her. Christ! She was too much. Too much for Jeff. He took me. I'll bet she was too much for my father. Maybe that's why he took off. She was a whore!"

The realization of what she had said blocked out everything for the moment. That she said it had to mean something. It had just come out.

"How do you feel?"

"Angry." That just came out too. But angry at whom, herself? Her mother?

"Magdalene's daughter," Doctor said.

"Oh, boy. I've got to sit up. I want to think. I don't want to just lie here kicking it around. I can't." She sat up and put her feet on the floor.

The doctor did not try to direct her. She sat with her eyes averted.

"I don't mean she was on the streets or anything like that, but there were men I pretended not to know about, even to myself. Like once when all the plumbing broke down at school and we were sent home early. She was supposed to be at work at the bookstore, but she wasn't. I heard them thumping in the bedroom and I went out again like lightning. I locked the door and went to a movie. *Who's Afraid of Virginia Woolf?* Oh, boy, was I a mess. I didn't ever want to go home so I went to the zoo. Those goddamn monkeys . . . It was like the whole cage was in heat. It wasn't just sex. All the kids at school were making out, and when I went on that peace march, it was great. It just happened and I hardly knew the boy. How many times have I told you this?"

"It comes up," Doctor said.

"One day we wouldn't have enough money to pay my tuition or the rent or something, and the next day it was okay. I was going to come out like a Vanderbilt. And I knew. I know what it was I hated most of all: she'd say to me, 'You know, it's all for you, my little darling. Everything I do . . .' And inside I'd be screaming. Outside I just said, Okay,

Mother. I believe you . . . Hey, that little child upstairs Juanita . . . a little Puerto Rican me." She told the doctor about Mrs. Rodriguez, then about Mack coming to look for Rita. "I told the police everything I knew about her except the part about you. I didn't mention you."

Doctor Callahan sat back in her chair, her feet elevated. The *New York Times* was on her side table. She touched her hand to it. "According to this, no one has seen her since Wednesday night. I saw her here Wednesday at six P.M."

"Good," Julie said. "I mean it's good that somebody saw her after you did."

"I understand."

"I'm very sorry, Doctor."

"Why?"

"I shouldn't have involved you."

The doctor looked at her quizzically. "Why don't we talk about that?" she said, and made that famous gesture with her hand that had the effect of toppling Julie over on the couch.

"I did ask myself why I was doing it—if it was because I really cared about her, or if it was a way of getting back to you. I think I was sincere when I said to you about a human being asking for help, you had to help them. But I did feel good about you and being able to tell her you would see her. It got me off the hook. Ah. All right. But why was I on the hook? What was she to me? I saw her take off her jacket . . . I went out of the shop and watched her go up the street toward Eighth Avenue. She took off her jacket and slung it over her shoulder. The way she walked was different, I felt she was turning back into a whore. No, I felt I'd been had. Put on. That's what I felt at first. Then she threw the jacket into the face of some guy"—Julie imitated the motion—"as though she was saying, No! I won't do it! And then she ran, and I couldn't see her. But you can bet I was cheering for her all the way. He dumped her jacket in a wastebasket and I thought for a minute I'd go and get it for her, but an old beggar woman got it before I'd even made up my mind. That's when I decided to call you. I believed her then. That's the main thing, and I thought, Even if I'm wrong, if she is a phony, Doctor will know it in ten minutes. And if she *is* a phony she still needs help."

"How do you feel now?"

"I want to believe in her. I do believe in her. By which I mean I don't think she killed Pete. But if I believe what I'm saying, then I've betrayed her all over the place. I've probably spoiled her chance of ever getting out."

"Isn't it possible you exaggerate your contribution?"

"I don't see how I could have done anything else. If she is innocent, maybe I can help prove that."

"What can you do?"

"A lot. I know things now about Pete I didn't know before."

"Was she the sick friend he mentioned in the note to you?"

"She could have been. She could have told him the same story she told me, about wanting to go home, et cetera, and he could have tried to help her."

"Was it through him you met her?"

"No, that was Mr. Bourke."

"Who is Mr. Bourke?"

"Well, Doctor, that's another story. Let's just say he's an all-around mutual friend."

"You have certainly acquired an odd assortment of friends in two weeks' time."

"There are lots more I haven't told you about—Detective Russo and Mrs. Ryan . . ."

"Will you continue in this shop? What do you call it?"

"Friend Julie's. Pete suggested Sister Julie." She sat up, remembering something that seemed important. "Mack called me Sister Julie. He did. 'Look, Sister Julie . . .'"

"Mack is the procurer?"

"Yes . . . It could be coincidence, his calling me Sister Julie. It sounds commoner than Friend Julie. But what if *he* got it from Pete?"

"We can stop there. I want you here Wednesday as usual."

"Don't worry, I'll be here."

"Don't worry? Is that what you mean, don't worry?"

"I guess I mean *do* worry."

"Why do you always guess?" Doctor let her chair up with a jolt. It was obviously a question for which she did not expect an answer at the moment.

Julie was halfway to the door when she remembered what

had pressed most on her mind, coming in that day. "Doctor, did Rita tell you the same things she said to me?"

Doctor Callahan looked as though she was not going to answer at all. Then she said, "She talked about herself. Wednesday at two."

Julie dared to persist. "Did you believe her?"

"It's never a matter of belief here. Patients often lie for a variety of reasons. Many times they don't even know they're lying. We can take that up sometime."

"What about Jeff? Am I to go to Paris?"

"Are you?" Doctor Callahan got to her feet and changed the paper towel on the pillow: a fresh towel for every patient.

"But what am I going to write to him?"

"You might send him the clippings from today's paper before his friends do."

16

"HAVE A GOOD DAY," the doorman said as Julie left Dr. Callahan's building. Like old times. Not quite. She'd never got Mother out in the open before. If she *was* out in the open. She kept disappearing. And why did she feel so angry? Doctor hadn't commented. Why are you angry? Because that's what I am, a Victorian spinster . . . That sure as hell wasn't Mother—that was Julie Hayes—"Dearest Jeff, a funny thing happened to me a couple of weeks ago when I left Dr. Callahan's office . . ." There was no point now in telling him of the interruption in therapy, unless his accountant called it to his attention, paying Doctor's bill. But where to begin? "In my last letter, I told you I was reading about Zoroaster . . ." Or: "Do you remember the revival of *Streetcar* we saw last year? The designer . . ." It seemed like a crazy patchwork of coincidences, and maybe it was in the beginning. The Tarot would say no, no accidents. If the Tarot had anything to do with it. She half-believed it did. Magdalene's daughter: that's where it began in earnest, when she wrote those words. Daddy, you bastard . . . Mother, you whore. It came up from the bowels of the couch like hidden treasure she had finally dug out. But that was not for Jeff, nor of Jeff. Or was it? "Dearest Jeff. I remember the talk you gave when I graduated and you got your honorary degree. You said, 'Get the facts, all the facts, and write them down before you start the story. Because if you don't, you'll find yourself making up facts as you need them. Your copy may be richer, but your reader will be ill informed, and you will have begun the corruption of history.' Aren't you impressed that I can recite that whole speech? I thought it was the most important speech I ever heard or read. I was in love!"

What? Oh, boy. Watch it, Julie . . ."The reason I mention it now, I want to give you the facts about the story in this morning's paper. I also know things which may not be facts, only feelings. I'd appreciate it if you would challenge me where you think I'm making up . . ." Hey? I mean it. *I do mean it.* Mrs. Julie Hayes of West Forty-fourth Street had identified the victim, according to the morning *Times*. No connection with Mrs. Geoffrey Hayes of West Seventeenth Street. But there is a connection. Make it or break it, Julie. Paris or bust.

A fine rain was falling. The park was a yellow mist, forsythia and pollution.

She took a bus, fetching a token out of her raincoat pocket. She kept a handful of tokens and loose change ready for transport, musical beggars, and Orange Julius, a beverage on which she often breakfasted at a stand on Fiftieth Street and Broadway.

On Forty-fourth Street she met Fritzie at one end of his leash with Juanita at the other, neither one of them doing what the other wanted. Outside the shop, Mrs. Ryan was standing under an umbrella, talking with the man from the telephone company, Mrs. Rodriguez counseling from her window.

"I said I'd be here by eleven-thirty," Julie said to the phone man. "Hi, Mrs. Ryan. Mrs. Rodriguez."

"Detective Russo told me ten sharp. You should get together. What kind of a telephone do you want?"

"The cheapest."

"Not if the city is paying for it, Julie," Mrs. Ryan advised.

"That'll be the day," Julie said and unlocked the door. She had to put her shoulder to it, stuck as it was, presumably with the dampness.

Mrs. Ryan gave a little cry. "Don't! Maybe there's a bomb."

"Come off it," Julie turned and used her backside and her heel. She supposed Mrs. Ryan and Mrs. Rodriguez had had quite a talk.

The door yielded and revealed a scattering of messages on the floor beneath the mail slot. She gathered them and took them to the card table in the back room. She told the phone installer that it would be all right to put the instrument where the last customer's phone had been connected.

"How long will it take?" Mrs. Ryan wanted to know.

"Ten, twenty minutes unless the rats have chewed up the wires."

"I'll come back," she said to Julie. "I waited till after twelve o'clock at McGowan's on Saturday night."

"Sorry.'

"I'm not reprimanding you, only saying I felt terrible because I didn't stay with you. Mrs. Russo says you've been a great help to the police."

Julie made a noise of agreement and looked at the messages. One was from Amy Ross, saying to call her at the Forum. A note on *Daily News* stationery was from a columnist, wanting an interview before two P.M. There were several throwaways. Another note, this one in a plain envelope addressed to "Friend Julie" and on stationery from which the letterhead had been torn away, read, "Please call me about Rita. 321-9270."

Mrs. Ryan was watching her from the inside doorway, hoping to be confided in. Julie put the messages beneath the crystal ball. Mrs. Ryan sniffed in disappointment and then made the best of the situation. "I'll bring us a little lunch . . . unless you want me to stay."

"That would be just fine—the lunch, thank you."

When Mrs. Ryan was gone, Julie read the note again, a heavy, childish hand which had taken great care. Somebody who did not want to go to the police? Mack?

She told the phone man she would be back in ten minutes and went out to ask Mrs. Rodriguez if she could come up and talk with her. Juanita was trying to tie a string around the neck of one of her dolls. She held it up to Julie for help. "Good dog." Julie couldn't remember her having put two words together before.

The *Daily News* was open on the table alongside the Rodriguez family photograph. Julie hadn't seen the morning edition. It carried a picture of Pete. He'd been wearing his hair longer when it was posed and his features were more delicate. You'd look twice to decide, male or female. Beautiful, but she didn't like it. To have got it into print so soon, the reporter probably dug it out of the paper's own morgue. There would have been a story with it when it first appeared.

"Your boy friend," Mrs. Rodriguez said and patted Julie's hand.

Julie let it stand that way. The more sympathy, the more information.

"The lady with the dog told me. He put up your curtains like a decorator. He don't look like that picture now."

He sure as hell didn't, but Julie knew what she meant. "Could I have the paper when you're through with it, Mrs. Rodriguez?"

"Here." She tore out the page and gave it to Julie. "The rest I keep. I don't read so quick in English."

Julie folded the paper and put it in her raincoat pocket. "Do you remember the young girl who came to see me last week? You said she was on the street. She didn't look it to me. How could you tell?"

"I could tell!" She was exasperated at being asked to explain something she couldn't explain. She gave a great wiggle to her ample body. "Something."

"Yeah. I thought maybe she'd been around before. Or since. Have you seen her again?"

"I don't see her, but I don't always look."

Not always. Just often.

"Was there anyone at all looking for me over the weekend?"

"Every once in a while somebody stops and looks in the window. I don't say anything. Yesterday I took Juanita on a ride on the ferry boat with her father."

"Nice. How about Mack?"

"Mack?" She made it sound like "Mock" and a total stranger.

"The guy with red hair, a dude, a pimp. You called him a gangster."

"I remember."

"Is he a gangster?"

"I don't know. He looks like a gangster, like she is a whore."

"Oh, for God's sake," Julie said, and then chanced to

catch the faintest look of satisfaction in Mrs. Rodriguez's eye. Satisfaction or relief? She stemmed her own impatience. It would get her nowhere. "Please, neighbor, my friend is dead. You don't like this Mack character any better than I do. Tell me what you can about him. I need to know."

Mrs. Rodriguez made a sour face. "It don't concern you."

"Please. I just want to know what he's like."

"No good. All right! I pay him money."

In her mind's eye Julie saw the child offering to give Mack back the coins he had thrown to her. But the mother? Then she caught on. "Blackmail?"

"Si. He finds out about me and Señora. He's trying to steal girls from Goldie, and so by accident he finds out." She rubbed her fingers against her thumb, the traditional sign of the payoff. "He comes for his percentage every week. So he don't tell Goldie."

"Oh, boy. Talk about a petty crook."

When Julie got downstairs again Juanita was whacking the make-believe dog on the sidewalk. Bad dog.

She watched the repairman dial and then hang up. The phone bell went off like a burglar alarm.

"It works," he said as though he had wrought a miracle.

Julie's first call was to Detective Russo, to tell him the phone had been installed. It was the pretext under which she could then ask him if anything new had developed.

"We're putting out an 'all points' on her and Mack. No sign of him in his usual haunts, and he has to be one of the last people in that apartment of hers. The one clean set of fingerprints in the place. That gal'd make somebody a good housekeeper."

Julie decided she'd better tell him about the note.

"Let me have it," Russo said. "I'll send somebody around to pick it up."

"Shall I try the number and see what happens?"

"Not till I say so."

Julie set up the typewriter, an old Underwood portable of Jeff's that had finished the major work of its lifetime before she had reached puberty. She sat a moment, her fingers on the keys, and in her fashion, vaguely Yoga, prayed that the energy Jeff transmitted through them would pass into her. A beginning, a middle, and an end, connecting all the way.

"Dearest Jeff, I am making a carbon copy of this letter because I need to write it for myself as well as you . . ."

She had almost finished a double-spaced page that got her no further than her meeting Mrs. Ryan outside Kanakas's Eighth Avenue shop when the woman walked in with the promised lunch in a paper bag.

"I left Fritzie home. I should never have let that child take him for a walk. He's all skittish and off his food."

Julie pushed the typewriter aside, turning it so the letter was facing the wall. "She's a spooky little kid. What do you make of the mother, Mrs. Ryan?"

"Well, now, Julie. I was going to ask you the same thing. I used to see her in church with her husband, a dapper little man she could carry under her arm. They say opposites attract . . ."

"At St. Malachy's?"

"No. There's a church on Forty-second Street I like to go to now and then. They say the Mass in Spanish and it sounds like Latin. I do miss the Latin Mass. I made egg salad sandwiches. I wasn't sure if you eat meat, so many young people don't nowadays."

"Egg salad's one of my favorites. Do you ever notice street characters, Mrs. Ryan? Hustlers and so forth?"

"I try not to, but yes, of course I do. I'm only human."

"Ever see a big white fellow with red hair, a flashy dresser? He crawls around in a red sports car that matches his hair."

"I have seen him, yes."

"Lately? Like over the weekend? Since Thursday, say."

"No, no. I couldn't say when, but I do know that when I did see him, I had the feeling I'd seen him before. Somewhere entirely different."

"You mean not on the street?"

Mrs. Ryan thought about it. "I can't really say. It's like something you almost have and then it goes up in smoke."

Julie was tempted to back off the question that came to her mind, but she asked it: "Would you have seen him anywhere with Pete?"

Mrs. Ryan's eyebrows went up and she pursed her lips.

Julie would have given a lot to have been able to track that stream of associations.

"I shouldn't think so."

"Meaning you don't want to think so."

"Well, I suppose that's so, and when you first asked, I said to myself, *Was* it? Something . . . Oh dear, I'm not much help, am I? When Laura Gibson was alive I was much more alert. She was such a vital body, even toward the end of her life, quick witted. She made a person think."

It was interesting that Laura Gibson had been cued in then. Julie took a bite of her sandwich and let Mrs. Ryan muddle through her memories. Her faded blue eyes were on the crystal ball, not that she was seeing it: it was simply in her line of vision. "Now isn't it strange, I've made a peculiar connection. When Laura finally had to go to the hospital, it was to St. Jude's and I do believe that's where I saw this Mack person."

Julie held her tongue. And her breath.

"He was ordering someone around," Mrs. Ryan went on tentatively. "Laura was having a spasm. I suppose he said, 'Get the doctor,' or something like it. I was just coming in the door so I didn't see much of it. I only guessed what was happening. Or maybe Peter told me."

"Was he there?"

"He was always there. Laura died holding onto his hand."

The question was, What was Mack doing there? Julie asked something she afterwards wished she hadn't: "Could Mack have been visiting one of the other patients?"

"It was a private room."

"Yeah," Julie said, feeling she had interrupted Mrs. Ryan's associations. Whatever Mack was doing in the hospital on that occasion, Pete would have known him from there, seeing him afterwards. They would almost certainly have had to meet on the street, in the vicinity, say, of Mr. Bourke's or even in the building where both Pete and Rita lived.

Mrs. Ryan was off on a reverie of her own. "We had such grand times in the Willoughby before that, Julie. Peter had a lovely voice, especially singing Irish songs or reciting poetry. My own father was an Irish rebel and the light of his life was Maude Gonne, a beautiful wild patriot for all that she was an aristocrat. She was the one Yeats wrote the play for that we seen the other night . . ." Speaking of the Irish, Mrs. Ryan became more Irish. "Sometimes the two of them would pretend at being Yeats and Maude Gonne," she went on, "him pouring out his heart in poetry and swearing he'd marry no woman if she wouldn't have him, and her saying she'd have no man until Ireland was free. It was a queer sort of make-believe between them, her and Peter. She never married, you know, but when she was younger, her affairs were legion. And Peter . . . We talked about that before, didn't we? Are you a Catholic, Julie?"

The question surprised her. Like a random shot and yet somehow it was relevant. "Can you be part Catholic, Mrs. Ryan?"

"No, dear. If you're part, you're all."

Julie shook her head. "My father was Irish and Catholic."

"Hayes," Mrs. Ryan said.

"That's my married name. I grew up with my mother's maiden name."

"Oh, dear. He was one of those, was he?"

"There were circumstances," Julie said.

"Don't be so sure. There is nothing annoys me more than the excuses women make for the weakness of Irish men. Have a part of my sandwich. You're skin and bones."

"No more, thank you. You eat it. It's very good."

"I'm not that fond of my own cooking. If you want more information about those days in the hospital, Julie, I know how we can get it. Sheila Brennan is an R.N. and lives at the Willoughby. It was her got Laura into St. Jude's in the first place. I'll find out when she's off duty and bring her around, shall I?"

"Do, and afterwards I'll buy us all a beer at McGowan's."

17

IT WAS ALMOST FOUR in the afternoon before Julie finished her letter to Jeff. She had been tempted several times to rewrite, having proposed at the outset that it be an orderly chronicle of the events, but the events evaded order. Or her mind did. Questions kept coming up which seemed as important as the incidents that prompted them. In the end, she decided that it was better to get everything on paper than to define "facts" arbitrarily without their qualifying circumstances. The decision might be a cop-out, but the ten-page letter gave her a veritable catalog of issues without answers. What it would give Jeff was something else.

What became apparent along the way was her own need to know. Her need. Absolutely. If she was going to understand Julie Hayes, understanding Pete Mallory was a part of it.

The letter had not been without interruptions. A female legman (legwoman?) for the columnist with the two P.M. deadline came by. Her boss had a great idea: Julie the occultist's premonition of the murder. No way. Several kids from the Forum stopped. She promised to join them later there and sent word with them to Amy Ross. She persuaded a customer that the next day would be more propitious for an inquiry of the cards.

Adding a postscript to the letter to say that she and Doctor Callahan had postponed the Paris decision for a session or two, she sealed the envelope, locked up shop, and walked to Thirty-fourth Street to mail it at the main post office.

Then she went to see Mr. Bourke. She remarked, going through the shop, that she had never seen a customer on the premises. He was tagging a group of lamps set apart, she guessed, for rental.

"Well, Julie. I didn't expect to see you."

"I don't know why not."

"The police and all. I figured they'd advise you to keep away."

"From what?"

Mr. Bourke sighed heavily. "Contamination. And they'd be right. I must've said it to you before: it's not a place for the likes of you. It wasn't a place for the likes of Pete either. I'll miss that boy in a way nobody's going to understand."

"I can try."

"Maybe you," Bourke said. A sad little droop of a smile.

"Have the police been here?"

"Time and again. What could I tell them that they don't already know? Not much they'd want to hear. I missed Pete at St. Malachy's yesterday. He was the lay reader. Do you know what that means?"

"I know. I'd heard him myself."

"Did you?" Bourke took off his glasses and polished them. "I've been going to that church for forty years. Every Sunday morning my mother and I used to sneak out of the house, leaving the old man to sleep it off, and go to Mass there. To this day, when I leave a church and dip my fingers in the holy water, I can see her reach out her hand and take a drop from mine." He crossed himself, telling it. "Afterwards, we used to go to the Mayflower Shop and have doughnuts and coffee. Pete and I often did the same thing. A half-hour. We never said much. It was . . . kind of a rest. For me anyway. There was something—I don't even know if it had to do with God. Peace, that's what it was about. If I could tell you, I would. You know what it was like? Forgiveness. Two people knowing and forgiving and yet never having to say a word about what."

What *did* you know? Julie wanted to ask. Forgive what? But she said, "Yeah."

"Well, God knows what happens now. At the moment, I don't care." He put his glasses on again, letting them slide down his nose almost at once.

"Did Pete really study to be a priest?"

"Not for long. His people were killed in a car accident and his sister was laid up from it for a long time. He took care of her and went to school part time, art school in Chicago. Then he blew the whole thing and ran away. Too much. Instead of getting better, she got more dependent on him. Like a marriage. He got to hate her and everybody else in the town where they kept saying he was such a good boy."

"Libertytown," Julie said.

"That's the place."

"Do you know Detective Russo?"

"Since he was that high." Bourke held his hand waist level.

"He talked to Pete's sister on the phone Saturday night. She was planning to come out to see the Irish Theatre Production."

"Did she tell the police that?"

Julie nodded.

"Even after she knew he was dead, she told it?"

"I think so."

Bourke shook his head. "She wouldn't have come. It was a game they played. Every few months Pete would say, 'I'm going to invite my sister out,' or 'I invited my sister to come and visit me. Where do you think I ought to take her, Philip, besides theater if I can find a play that won't shock her?' They talked about it on the telephone, him and his sister, how he was coming on such and such a date, but she never did come to see him."

"That's wild."

"I suppose it is, but I can understand it. They were probably closer that way than living together."

Oh, boy. Paris or bust.

"When did you first get to know him, Mr. Bourke?"

"I've been trying to think. I must have met him two or three years ago at the Willoughby. There'd be a party at Miss Gibson's—or Mrs. Ryan's. When they'd get feeling good, they'd invite anybody who came along. Like myself. She was a very gracious lady, Miss Gibson. Then after she died, I got to know him better. While she was sick, he'd come in sometimes and talk. And after she died, he'd just come in."

"How was he able to pay her hospital bills?"

"I don't know that."

A cutoff, Julie thought. Too quick. She should not have asked so directly. "But he did, you know."

"I'm not surprised. Now I've got to get these lights together, Julie. They'll be picking them up in an hour or so."

An hour or so was going to be six o'clock. The moonlighters: without whom, as he had told her himself, he could not stay in business.

"About Rita, Mr. Bourke. Did you know she lived in the same building as Pete?"

"Not till I read it in the paper."

"Did you ever see them together?"

"I think I may have introduced them, Julie. A couple of months ago. The vice boys came out full force that night and Rita ducked in here. Pete was here and she asked him if he would do her a favor. She changed clothes in the can in back and he walked out with her. She had one of those knitting bags and he even carried it for her. Half the gals on the street were busted that night. Not her."

"Was she ever busted?"

"Not that I know of. She hadn't been around long then, but she was a pro."

"I was just thinking, she knew how to take care of herself in an emergency, didn't she?"

"You're damn right. I resented what she done that night, picking Pete up like that."

"Did you like her? Feel sorry for her? What?"

"Nothing like that." He thought about it for a minute. "What you're asking me, Julie, is why I let her come in here in the first place."

"All right."

"Because I was afraid of Mack and he was the one decided I was going to be her shelter."

"I get it," Julie said, but she didn't, not all of it. "What could he do to you?"

"I don't want to find out."

"Has he got other rackets besides prostitution?"

"I have no idea. Why don't you leave police work to the police?"

"You're right," Julie said. She was only making him more uptight.

To appease her or something like that he said, "How about that book you were going to lend me?"

"I'll try and remember next time around." She didn't think she was ever going to loan Mr. Bourke that or any book. That notion had come out of another era when she thought everybody was as innocent as she had thought Rita.

By the time Julie got to the Forum Amy had gone, but she had left a note on the message board: "The Master says no memorial here. So that's that." The Master was the director of the Forum. "I left out some scrapbooks for you in the library you might like to look at. If you want to call me at home tonight, here's my number . . ."

The stories Amy had marked concerned theater productions in which Pete had been involved. In all the clippings the names of members of Actors Forum had been underlined, the reason for the scrapbooks in the first place. A review of the Street Theater Festival carried the picture of Pete that had appeared in that morning's *Daily News.* "The New York Street Theater troupe took their caravan last night to a vacant lot on Houston Street, the gateway to Little Italy. They set theater back four hundred years. Is that bad? Not as seen by this reviewer. I should think they modeled their wildly improvisational happening on the classic *Commedia dell'Arte* with something for everybody in the family. Pratfalls, mime, political satire all combined to make an hour's hilarious entertainment. Take the balcony scene from *Romeo and Juliet:* 'O, Romeo, Romeo, wherefore art thou Romeo? Deny thy father and refuse they name . . . what do you mean, deny my father, refuse my name? I am proud to be an Italian!'

"The genius of this troupe seems to be Peter Mallory who mounted the production and acts as stage-manager-narrator . . ."

Julie wrote down the names of the Forum members in the cast. One of them, Rudy Farber, had done Julie's audition

123

scene with her which had won her membership in the Forum. She hadn't seen him since, but she had meant to. He had caught on as a nightclub comic and she was pretty sure he was still playing at The Guardian Angel in the Village.

18

"BABY, we were as rotten as a couple of two-month eggs,"
Rudy said of the audition scene.

"Then how come I got into the Forum?"

"Charm . . . and a successful marriage." The comic smiled
puckishly.

"You mean I got in because I was married to Geoffrey
Hayes?"

"It didn't harm."

"But it's not supposed to be that way."

Rudy mocked her, a musical flourish, "Da-dah."

"Jeff couldn't care less."

"Still married to him?"

"Of course."

"Don't give me of course. There ain't no such condition.
If you want to tell me about yourself, that's okay, but don't
make it sound like I'm undermining the holy institution of
matrimony."

"There's nothing to tell. I didn't come to talk about me."

"About me?" He said it jokingly. "Look at the company
I'm keeping these days. Look!" He flung out his hands to
call attention to the walls of his dressing room. They were
crowded with the photographs of nightclub entertainers.
Generations of them. Julie sat on the foot locker he had
turned on its end for her alongside his dressing table and
looked from face to face as he called their names like an
honor roll. Not many of them meant much to Julie. "They
all got their start at The Guardian Angel. I sure as hell
wasn't going to make it in theater, so I got myself a uniform"
—he nodded at the costume hanging behind the door, over-
alls, a blue denim shirt, and a straw hat—"and a partner.

125

He's the brains of the act, the brains, the soul. It's like this: He's the persona, I'm the personality."

"Okay."

"I'll introduce you." He reached across the cluttered table and touched her hand. "Pete Mallory: you want to talk about him?"

She nodded.

Rudy looked like a "Rudy," a round, mischievous face with a large, mobile mouth and restless eyes that came back unexpectedly and took hold of yours, then wandered off again. "How did he get tied up with a hooker, will you tell me that?"

Tied up. "What do you mean, tied up?"

"Tied up," he repeated and shrugged.

"Hookers are pretty casual acquaintances, right?"

"You got a point. What did I mean? Pete was one of those semper fidelis guys. Semper fidelis—that's Marine Corps for Be Prepared. No, seriously, he either got involved or he didn't. He had a reputation for running out on people, but the fact is, he never ran out on anybody he was committed to. He'd cut out before, not after. So I guess I meant just what I said, tied up.

"Pete came down here when we opened. The act is his kind of theater. I don't talk. I mime whatever comes into my mind while Hutch strums the guitar and sings his crazy country folk stuff. I took it right out of Pete's street theater . . . Oh, Julie. I loved the bastard." His mouth spread in a wide smile that came to a sad conclusion, his lower lip sticking out. He looked at his watch. "I'm going to start putting on my makeup. I'm a slow dresser."

"Tell me when you want me to leave."

"I will. Want to see the show?"

"Yes."

"I like that about you, Julie. Straight. No sugary crap."

"Did you know Laura Gibson?"

"Sure. A real trooper, but she couldn't play the star game. And she couldn't play with phonies, which when you come right down to it most actors are. I mean when the company was bad, she was lousy."

126

"What about her and Pete? Were they lovers, friends, what?"

Those restless eyes of the comic settled on Julie's. "For private or public consumption?"

"For me. I want to understand."

He looked in the mirror while he smeared cream on his face and then wiped it off. "I think she brought Pete out. I know damn well she did. He was hung up on his mother or his sister—some Freudian knot that Miss Gibson took into her clever fingers and dissolved like a cat's cradle. I was pretty tuned in on the action and old Laura knew it. She played Pete like an instrument, and I don't think he ever got that from anybody else—or wanted it.

"After she'd get a few drinks in her—she was a great boozer: she used to say, 'I've devoted my life to the three Bs —Bed, Booze, and the Boards'—anyway, after a couple of drinks, she'd sit with her hand on mine and tell me what a wonderful lover he was."

"I don't think I like her much," Julie said.

"She could be a bitch, but she was a lot of other things, too. She was somebody you always had to help get started. Then she was great. She could take over then and pull the whole thing together—on stage and off."

"Yeah." It tied in with Julie's memory of her in *Streetcar*.

"Wrap it all up, and I'd have to say that was the best experience I ever had as an actor. The whole package was Pete's idea—and hers, I guess. He'd just shook loose of Ira Windsor and that old-fashioned formal, fixed idea of design. The *set* piece, you know? Frozen. Money. You want to hear this?"

"You bet."

Rudy looked at his watch again. "What he set out to do was a composite of theater—old-style—folk—improvisation. The way he started was by going into the neighborhoods himself—walking, eating, drinking, playing with the kids, talking to cops, the whole scene. Remember, Lindsay was mayor and Fun City hadn't gone bust. Pete got carte blanche. We did the wedding scene from a play called *The Dybbuk* in Jewish neighborhoods—my God, half the street

127

got into the beggars' dance. Then there was *Cathleen ni Houlihan* for the Irish."

"I know that part," Julie said.

"Laura Gibson, wow."

"Yeah."

"And Little Italy—that's where I came into my own. What you see me do tonight, that's where it started. It was like a Fellini circus, only . . . ours."

"I read a review," Julie said.

"Pete was the M.C.—a white suit and a whip. Ha! Let me get through here and I'll tell you a funny thing that maybe wasn't as funny as I thought it was."

Julie watched him redden his lips, put dots in the corners of his eyes, and enlarge upon the already large mouth. He darkened his eyebrows and peaked them into a shape of perpetual wonder.

"What a way to make a living, yeah? I say it every night along about now, looking at this damn fool in the mirror. Then I thank God. I make people laugh and it's the most wonderful feeling in the world . . . next to sex."

Julie wondered why he had added that last jarring phrase. Then she thought she knew: he was embarrassed at the admission of wonder at the miracle of his own talent. The cover.

"There was a guy in the audience—it was in a vacant lot on Houston Street—who got a crush on Pete. Mafia, maybe. But from then on, wherever we were playing, this guy would show up with his bodyguards, a couple of klunks you'd just call bodies.' He had a kind of cherubic look, a little boy face. The night we closed on Houston Street he gave the whole company a party at the Paradise Restaurant. Never said a word to anybody that I know of, just sat and looked at Pete. No advances, nothing. Whenever he wanted anything, one of his boys took care of it. You know, from the waiters—from the limousine, a big black Caddie. We got to calling him The Little King."

"Who was he?"

"Don't know. Never did."

"How did Pete react?"

"He played it cool. Like it was all in the script. Only there wasn't any script, of course, just the outline which he fed us every night. But let me tell you this. Then I'll get the boss in and introduce you. He used to walk out through the audience with that whip and this once, when he'd just passed Baby Face, he turned and cracked the whip. You never saw anybody go into such ecstasy as The Little King. Instant orgasm. His boys stood there like bulldogs on leashes, but they never made a move. Pete went straight through the crowd back to the truck and put the whip away. He wasn't supposed to be through, but he was. When I finished my routine I went looking for Pete and found him with Laura in the portable dressing room. He was on his knees, his head smack against her belly, and her soothing and hugging him and saying it was going to be all right."

The club was crowded. The manager smiled a lot, but he could not quite conceal his irritation at having to find a place for Julie. "You won't have a table to yourself, miss. We're very busy."

"That's good," Julie said. "I mean I'm glad business is good."

He took a long look at her, his expression suggesting that he might be about to tell her something almost intimate, say, that her lipstick was on crooked. Julie looked at him as frankly. He put her in mind of some of the old-time show people who lived at the Willoughby: you couldn't guess their age. Which didn't matter because they weren't their age anyway, being both very young and very old at the same time. He went off without saying any of the things that seemed to be on his mind.

Julie ordered a hamburger at four dollars and a massive Coke.

When the show was about to start, a man in a dinner jacket slipped into the other chair at the table. He sat with his arms folded, massaging his biceps while his eyes roamed the house. He had to be a watchdog or bouncer of some sort. He and Julie exchanged brief smiles. He spoke to her just as the M.C. came on stage. "Sweets Romano's the guy you're looking for."

Julie repeated the name. She had heard it before, but

she could not remember where. "How do I find him?"

He gave an enormous shrug: what a stupid question. "Look him up."

Having introduced "Hutch and Rudy," the M.C. came to the table. Julie's erstwhile companion gave him his chair. It was the house table. The M.C. sat with his eyes closed.

Sweets Romano . . . the guy you're looking for. Julie hadn't known she was looking for any guy. Rita, yes. Possibly Mack. Then she made the connection. Russo had told the Homicide detective in the car that Saturday night that Mack's record included assault, drugs . . . and that he was tied up with the Romano outfit. To volunteer this information, these nightclub people had to know she was receptive to it, looking for it. And that had to mean someone had listened in on her conversation with Rudy. Baby Face . . . The Little King: Sweets Romano. The images matched somehow.

Julie wanted out. But to run was ridiculous. They'd know she would take the message to the police. It was probably what they wanted. Why? She ate her hamburger and tried to keep her mind on the Hutch and Rudy Show. It was no use.

She told Rudy he was marvelous when he stopped after the act and kissed the top of her head. He introduced his partner and then slyly snatched her check from the table. As soon as the comics had left the floor, Julie took off.

The bouncer opened the door for her. "A cab, Mrs. Hayes?"

Mrs. Hayes. Everybody knew everybody. "No thanks. I'll manage."

On the street she flagged down the first cruising taxi. She tipped the driver extravagantly and asked him to wait until she had closed the vestibule door behind her.

The more lights she turned on in the apartment, the more eerie and silent it seemed. She had intended to call Detective Russo, but the thought of her own voice reinforcing her aloneness made her put off the call until morning. She went quickly to bed leaving most of the lights on.

19

RUSSO WAS IN A MEETING when Julie called in the morning, but he sent word that he would like her to stop by the station house when she came uptown. She arrived in time to see a procession of prostitutes and arresting officers take off for court. Some of the women looked Julie over with a cold eye. New girl in town.

Russo's meeting broke up a few minutes after her arrival. He came out of the captain's office with a number of other detectives, Lieutenant Donleavy among them. The Homicide man tipped his hat to Julie and said, "We're going to have to put you on the payroll, little lady."

Russo took her upstairs to the room in which he had taped her statement after she had identified Pete's body. He handed her a flyer smelling of fresh ink. Rita as composed by the police artist.

"Hey." Julie was impressed by its accuracy.

"I told you," Russo said.

"Do you still think she's in New York?"

"No. I think I was wrong about that. Last Thurday she bought a great big teddy bear at F.A.O. Schwarz. How about that? I owe you a drink. Remember? You gave me the tip."

"I remember."

"Then along about five that afternoon she was seen at the bus terminal."

"So she did go home."

"I'd like to talk to someone who saw her on the bus before I'd say that, but it looks that way."

"Have you found Mack?"

"We will."

131

Julie said, "Am I right that you told Lieutenant Donleavy he was part of the Romano outfit?"

"He used to be, but they've been dumping the crude numbers like him since they went respectable. They're very heavy in real estate nowadays, most of it lawyer-fronted, fancy corporation names. But I wouldn't be surprised if Mack hustles his whores into family-owned buildings."

"I think Pete may have had a connection with somebody called Sweets Romano," Julie said.

Russo thought about it. "It fits."

"How?"

"Tell me your story first. Shall we turn on the machine?"

"All right."

When Julie finished he said, "Nobody sees much of Sweets these days. He's supposed to have gone in for collecting culture. But how about this: he's also an entrepreneur of Grade B movies. In other words, porn films."

"Is that what you meant, it fits?"

"Doesn't it?"

"I can't see Pete in that scene. I just can't. He was half-priest, for God's sake."

"And the other half?"

She shrugged. "Artist. Yeah, artist."

"I'm a square cop, Julie, but I don't think there's any reason to make those things except for money. Not if the guy's honest about it, and I know you're going to tell me he was honest."

"Pete did need money once, a lot of it. When Laura Gibson was dying, he took care of her. He paid her bills, doctors, hospital . . ." She stopped: Mrs. Ryan had put Mack into the hospital scene.

"Once." Russo picked up the word. "Don't hit me for this, but does anybody ever need money just once?"

"Yeah. Pete."

"Okay, if you say so." The detective sped up the tape and when it was run through he removed, boxed, and labeled it. "Donleavy's going to love this. You should've heard him this morning—'Dig! Goddamn it, dig!' Family history, the works. Have you been in touch with Mallory's sister?"

"No," Julie said, "but I will call her. What about Pete's body?"

"It'll go home soon."

"And the lab report?"

"That doesn't have anything to do with it."

"Is it in?" Julie persisted.

He nodded. "Inconclusive."

"Come on, Detective Russo. What does that mean?"

"There was semen, but that doesn't prove of itself he had sex. The discharge could have happened during death trauma."

"Okay." She had asked for it.

"We just don't know what went on there. Everything's screwy—the business of no key, the place as neat as a pin, except for the one area. One set of fingerprints, Mack's, with all the johns coming and going? That's crazy. Mack paid the rent there, even before she moved in. That was two months ago. Mallory lived in the building for five years. Who owns the building? I wouldn't be surprised now if it was the Romano syndicate. But what was going on between your friend and the little prostitute—I wish I knew."

"If anything," Julie said.

"She's traveling light, wherever she is. She gave most of her clothes to a thrift shop after first trying to sell them there; she made up a cock-and-bull story about getting married to a third-world diplomat, whatever the hell that is . . ."

"No kidding," Julie said. She asked the name of the thrift shop. Haven House.

"I'll tell you one thing, Julie. I'm glad my job is collecting hard, cold evidence. I don't go in for the psycho bit."

Julie wondered what had brought that on.

Then: "Donleavy trying to figure out what it could mean, a whore buying a teddy bear. She wanted a present for her kid brother, right?"

"Right."

He shook his head. "It sure makes you wonder."

"What?"

"What the brass looks for when they go over the promotions list."

Julie did not much like that recurring confidence. And Donleavy was more her style, by the sound of it. She made no comment.

Russo returned to business. "What I thought we'd do this morning, Julie, I'd like you to try that phone number from here where we can put it on tape. Identify yourself and see what comes across. The phone is listed to a May Weems on Fifty-second Street. Mack's her pimp. Or was at the time of her last arrest. Don't tell her you know her name, of course."

Julie did not especially want to make the call, but she saw no reason not to. "What am I to say to her?"

"Just what you'd say to anybody who left a message for you to call them. Who are you? What do you want? But keep her talking."

"Okay."

Russo got the line he wanted and dialed. He handed the phone to Julie before the first ring. She assumed the recording device was operating.

The third ring brought an answer. " 'Lo?" Sweet and low.

"This is Julie Hayes. I have a message to call this number."

"Friend Julie?"

Julie and Russo exchanged glances. "That's me."

"I was hoping you could help me get in touch with my friend Rita," the woman said, clearing her throat and then speaking with a certain hesitation that might be natural to her or might indicate that there was someone with her.

"I was hoping you could tell me," Julie said.

Russo made a sign to go easy.

The woman gave a surprised "Huh?" Then: "Don't you know where she is? She said like you'd sent her to this place. And I was thinking, why couldn't I go there too."

"Sorry, I can't help you," Julie said.

Russo made a winding sign: keep talking.

"Rita didn't mention having a friend," she tried.

"We was real close, Rita and me."

"How close? I mean were you in-laws or something?"

134

"Wife-in-laws. Know what that means?"

"Sure."

"Only now I want to split too, divorce like."

"Can't help you," Julie said.

Russo shook his head. This was not the way he wanted it played. Julie had the feeling that May might just know more than she did herself. If she did, Julie wanted to find out, but not on police tape, in case it involved Doctor Callahan.

"All I want is the name of the halfway house," May said before Julie could head her off.

"I don't have any such," Julie said and hung up the phone. A halfway house: that had to be Doctor Callahan's idea, and if there was a particular one, that too was Doctor's recommendation. She faced a detective who was both surprised and angry. "I'm sorry, Detective Russo, but I don't like to be used by anybody, including the police."

"What did she say? It's on the tape if you don't want to tell me."

"Nothing, really. I advised Rita when she came to see me," Julie lied, "to find herself a place to stop off part-way home, some place where she could get used to the idea that she wasn't a prostitute anymore. She must have told this May person. May wanted to know where it was." Much too much explaining.

"And is there a place?"

"It was only a figure of speech," Julie said, and realizing that he would listen to the exact words anyway, she repeated them, hoping thereby to make them seem less specific, "a halfway house. That's what they call drug rehabilitation centers, isn't it?"

"Is it? Julie, it was you gave me the number of Miss Weems, if you don't want to play square with the police, don't volunteer to play at all. Now I've got work to do. Thanks for coming in."

"Don't mention it." There was no use trying to fix things. Unless she was prepared to mention Doctor Callahan. She wasn't.

He walked her down the stairs in silence. Then, as she

was leaving: "You'd better count on it: Miss Weems is fronting for Mack. He's the one who's looking for the half-way house with Rita in it. It may turn out he wants Rita worse than we do."

20

"THANKS FOR COMING IN," Julie thought, pounding her heels on the sidewalk of Ninth Avenue. Belatedly, she was furious with Russo. Thanks for coming in. She had brought him a direct link among Romano, Pete, and Mack, something it might have taken him a week to turn up without her help. She wasn't even sure he was glad to have the information. Maybe he didn't want the Romano connection: big in real estate. Rita was more his speed. Julie was swinging in all directions and it did not take her long to realize that Russo was not the actual object of her anger: she was. She had herself to blame now if Doctor became involved, playing police lady, first assistant to a detective third grade. Whoops. Another twist to the umbilical of truth: with his "psycho" crack, Detective Russo had alienated Friend Julie.

She had to turn back to look for Haven House. Rita's fantasy of being married to a third-world diplomat was wild; her notion of the third world could not be much deeper than Julie's own and the first thing that came to mind with the phrase was the prevalence of black people. Which, on the surface, made it hard to reconcile the fantasy marriage with Rita's remark, made it hard to reconcile the fantasy marriage with Rita's remark—concerning Goldie—that she didn't think she could fall in love with a black man. Julie wondered if, asking questions in the thrift shop, she should try to pass as a police investigator. She was about to go public for the first time.

The woman in charge of the shop—run for the benefit of a school for the severely retarded—looked as though she were an alumna of Miss Page's School. "Can I help you, dear?"

All right.

"Well, yes," Julie said, and tuned her own accent to the prevailing key. "Detective Russo said you might be kind enough to repeat for me the story Rita Morgan told you. He wants my psychological evaluation of it."

"Rita Morgan. Ah, yes. The unfortunate." Undoubtedly a Miss Page graduate. With a straight "A" in Compassion.

The one customer in the shop, a teen-aged girl, slipped out the door with a surreptitious glance over her shoulder. "What did she steal?" Julie said.

"I'm afraid you're right. Probably a bit of costume jewelry. I follow them sometimes and ask them to pay a token price—I'll ask for anywhere between a nickel and a quarter."

"Killjoy."

"You *are* joking?"

"You bet . . . Try to remember from the first time Rita Morgan came in the store."

"She only came once."

"But she tried first to sell you certain items of apparel?"

"Yes . . . some exquisite lingerie which had never been worn. She said she was going to be married and it was part of her trousseau, but her husband-to-be wouldn't understand such finery. He was a third-world diplomat, she said. But it was rather curious, Miss . . . Mrs. I don't even know your name."

"Mrs. Julie Hayes. Please don't stop about Rita. It was curious, you say."

"Curious . . . yes. When I asked if he was with the U.N. she didn't seem to understand. I know now of course that it was a complete fabrication."

"That doesn't matter," Julie said. "It's the fabrication that interests me. I think we reveal more of ourselves in the lies we tell than we do when we try to tell the truth."

"For me it's quite the opposite. I don't find it all that difficult to tell the truth, and I can't lie worth a darn."

Julie smiled and prompted gently, "A third-world diplomat."

"She said that in his country only women of the street wore fancy underclothes and she wanted to do everything proper when he took her home. I explained that we have no purchasing budget, and when I think now of what she said, well . . . she said, 'I don't mind donating—if they're going to bring a good price to somebody.' I said I'd save them for the summer auction and that seemed to please her. And, of course, I offered to send her the usual tax-deductible receipt. You can imagine how foolish I felt telling that to Detective Russo when I found out what her real occupation was."

"What did she say?"

"That please, I wasn't to send any receipt. She didn't want to have to explain it to her fiancé. She also left a box which included two lamé dresses, a gold one and a silver. She was gone by the time I got around to opening the box. I did wonder, such a child for clothes like that."

Julie nodded. "Any more conversation?"

"She wanted to know what severely retarded meant as against just plain retarded, and I explained it meant people for whom there was no hope that they would ever be able to help themselves. 'But they don't know there isn't any hope, do they?' she said. And I told her what I believe is so: If they knew, they wouldn't be severely retarded and there'd be hope. It sounds like semantics, and maybe it is, but to me it's worth saying because it sounds cheerful. She smiled when I said that, I do believe gratefully. She said, 'My brother is retarded.' "

Julie held back any show of surprise.

"And that too," the woman added, "could be something she made up."

"It could, couldn't it?"

Julie went along to Forty-fourth Street and wrote down Rita's account of herself as given to the thrift shop woman. Why that story? Why any story? And the retarded brother for whom she bought a teddy bear the next day, and then got as far at least as the Port Authority Building . . . a couple of hours before Pete Mallory was murdered in her apartment. She wanted to do everything proper when the third-world diplomat took her home. Psychological evaluation. Yeah.

The morning papers carried Sergeant Greenberg's sketch of Rita. That was going to be a great help when it came to doing everything proper. The third world. Suppose Rita meant The Life as one world, the straight world as number two, and a kind of limbo as number three, a halfway house . . . Hey! Then who was the diplomat? Pete?

Julie locked the shop door so that she would not be disturbed and phoned the Illinois area code for Libertytown Information. She got the number of Helen Mallory and dialed it before she could change her mind. Waiting, listening to the bleeps and buzzings in the few seconds before the connection was completed, she thought of Russo's picture: the lone woman groping her way through the house to answer the phone in the middle of the night. Did she look like Pete? Younger? Older? The phone was ringing. The voice that answered was strong and resonant. Somehow Julie had expected a mouse.

"Miss Mallory?"

"Yes."

"My name is Julie Hayes and I'm calling from New York. I'm a friend of your brother's and I've been wanting to call you and offer my condolences."

"I don't remember Peter's mentioning you, but I do thank you."

Strong and resonant, but a groaner. Julie wanted to say, He didn't mention you much either, but she said, "I was supposed to meet him the night he was found."

"Oh, you're the one. I should offer you condolences then too."

"Thank you," Julie said. "Are you going to come to New York?"

"I don't expect to now. Pete kept trying to get me to visit him. It would be awful for me with him not there anymore."

"If you want me to help you with Pete's things, packing them and sending them on, I will."

"That's real kind of you, but Father Doyle is going to take care of that for me. Were you and Pete engaged?"

"Engaged?" Julie repeated, wanting to be sure, and wanting a second or two to weigh the idea and where it came from.

"Engaged to be married."

"No. We were only friends. I'm already married. I don't think Pete was actually engaged to anyone, Miss Mallory."

140

She could think of no other way to play for more information.

"I'm glad to hear that. I wouldn't want to think there was someone who didn't get in touch with me."

"Pete was probably teasing you," Julie said. Her palms were wet with the tension of trying to coax information without asking directly. Why not ask directly? Something told her not to. The subject might close forever.

"Well, it did sound a little like that, like he wanted to see what my reaction would be. We were terribly close, you know, for brother and sister."

"I understood that," Julie said.

"What did he tell you about me?" the sister asked.

To lie or not to lie? With the truth according to Mr. Bourke, she decided. "Only that you were close—after your parents' death—and your injuries."

"Did he tell you I'm lame?"

"No."

"He used to carry me down the stairs every morning and up the stairs every night. He cooked and washed for me. Completely devoted."

Oh, boy.

"And then he went away so that I'd learn to be self-reliant. And I did. Oh, yes, I learned. I was going to come to New York to see those Irish plays. Our mother was Irish. A saintly woman, by the values Pete and I were brought up to respect. Well, I shouldn't run up your phone bill, Mrs. Hayes . . ."

"Do. I can afford it really. If it's important and sometimes it is, just to talk. Please call me Julie."

"If you call me Helen."

"I will. Helen, what did Pete say about being engaged?"

"He didn't say that. He said something like, 'What if I was to come home—what if I *were* to come home with a brand-new wife?' "

Julie waited. So did Helen Mallory. Finally Julie said, "I didn't know Pete had been married ever."

"Well, I think it was only a manner of speaking."

"Yes, I see. Of course."

"Julie, do you know the woman where the police found his body?"

"She's a young girl. I met her a couple of times. She's disappeared now. I don't have anything to go on, but I keep wondering if she doesn't come from Libertytown."

"I never heard of her. The police asked me on the phone, and Sheriff Anderson out here. Rita Morgan."

"That might be her stage name," Julie said, forgive me actor of the world. "The sheriff will probably bring you a picture soon. It looks a lot like her."

"Is she a fallen woman?"

"I wouldn't say that," Julie said. Helen sounded biblical.

"I work in the office of our local paper, the *Weekly Chronicle*," Helen said, "and that's what my boss said it sounds like."

"Maybe," Julie conceded and changed the subject. Rita was not going home anywhere now without the stigma. "If you want to call me for anything, Helen, please do. Let me give you my number here at the shop and at home."

Miss Mallory repeated the numbers. "What kind of work do you do, Julie?"

"I'm a private investigator. Or I will be as soon as I get my license."

21

THE CRACK IN DOCTOR'S CEILING was definitely getting bigger. Julie wondered if any of her patients ever thought of hiding things in it.

"When I was a kid I used to hide things in the sofa, peanut shells, paper clips, vitamin pills that tasted awful, The Pill . . . I'm only kidding about The Pill. I'll have to start taking it again if I go to Paris. Isn't it funny, I just said it when I was thinking of hiding things? . . . Maybe I won't take it and take my chances on getting pregnant. Except if I had a child, I'd want to want it really. I mean, I'd want it to know it was wanted. I'll say that for my mother, she made me know she'd wanted me. Even if my father didn't. Mrs. Ryan was funny about Irish women always making excuses for the men. I wonder why Mother told me. I mean she could just as easily have said he died, you know. I think if it'd been me, I'd have got an urn of some sort and put it on the piano or the mantel or someplace and said, That's your father, Julie. Pay respect. Except him being a Catholic, cremation would be out. But I wouldn't even have had to know he was a Catholic. Hey, maybe down deep she hoped I'd go looking for him someday. I'd find him and I'd say, Well now, Mr. Hayes, let me introduce myself. Look me over and tell me, do you still want out? Why did she tell me, doctor?"

"Why do you think?"

"To make herself look better to me, raising me without him? Wouldn't it be crazy if she made the whole thing up? If there wasn't ever an Irish diplomat named Thomas Francis Mooney? God! What a joke . . ."

"You just said, *Mr. Hayes,* let me introduce myself."

"Mr. Hayes . . . Did I say that? Jeff is almost old enough

. . . Oh, Doctor, a million things exploding—thoughts. I can't hang onto them . . ."

"Take your time and tell them as they come."

"The church and Pete and me being jealous, the whore of Babylon, I always liked that—the Roman Catholic Church—the whore of Babylon—Mother, Jeff . . . my saying she was a whore. Sure there were men but that doesn't mean she was, there weren't that many, I was exaggerating . . . I was jealous of her, that's what it was all about . . . I wanted Jeff for myself and it was like she wanted him too. And then I did get him mixed up with my father. Does that make sense?"

"If it makes sense to you."

"It's like he's always somewhere else where he doesn't want me and then when he does, I don't want him. I don't know. It's all mixed up."

"It doesn't have to be."

"It's like I want it that way, like I'd have to do something if it wasn't . . ."

"Such as?"

"Grow up, stop blaming everybody else, stop pretending to be a little girl, an angry kid . . . I keep saying I'm not a little girl, but when Pete said I'd be one at seventy-five it was like he knew me better than I did . . . I wonder if he knew Rita, really knew her. I don't know why I keep thinking he was so wise, maybe I think all men are, the very idea of diplomat, of newspaper correspondent . . ."

"Why do you think your mother told you about this Thomas Francis Mooney?"

"She couldn't have made that name up, could she?"

"Why not?"

"I mean it's corny Irish. And boy, can they be corny. No, his name is on the records, my birth certificate, et cetera, and I do feel at home with the Irish, Doctor. I do."

"And you don't in your own home?"

"I don't feel like it's mine. That picture of Jeff in the living room . . ."

"Painted by his first wife?"

"Yeah."

"Why don't you ask him to remove it?"

"I'd have to admit I was jealous or something."

"Is that so terrible?"

"But I'm nobody and she's a painter. I don't have the right . . ."

"You're Julie Hayes, the present Mrs. Geoffrey Hayes."

"The former . . . who? Hey, I'll bet Jeff could find out about my father."

"Can't you find out, if you do want to know? Aren't you playing the great detective these days?"

"Am I? You could say that. Absolutely. I told Pete's sister on the phone that I was a private investigator. Ha! I also told someone I was making a psychological evaluation of Rita's behavior for Detective Russo." She looked round at the doctor.

"That was brave of you," Doctor said dryly, and with a flip of her hand directed the patient's head forward.

"Now how about this? Talk about diplomats. Rita made up this story to tell the woman in the thrift shop where she tried to sell all her fancy clothes."

"A third-world diplomat," Doctor said after Julie repeated the woman's story. "What an interesting fantasy."

"I have a theory about where it came from."

"Had you told her about yourself, your natural father?"

"No. It's spooky though, her latching onto an imaginary diplomat."

"What does the word *diplomat* suggest to you?"

"Someone who makes peace, who negotiates. Somebody patient, polished, polite . . . I don't think my mother made him up."

Doctor said, "But Rita did make up her fiancé and chose a diplomat, someone who makes peace, who negotiates—that's a fairly general concept."

"I think she was talking about Pete underneath. It's just even possible that Pete *was* going to marry her." Julie turned her head quickly and surprised the look of incredulity on Doctor Callahan's face. "All right, Doctor it's not all that far out. I talked to Pete's sister on the phone yesterday. She's kind of weird too. Who isn't? I mean I was lying in bed last night thinking about that conversation and what I'd heard about them from Mr. Bourke, but what came up, you know, was how the people in Libertytown would feel about Helen.

And about Pete, and I'll bet those good straight Americans would say, Didn't the Mallory children turn out fine when you consider how they lost their parents when they were only teen-agers? You and I see the quirky insides of people, Doctor. But there's Helen Mallory going to work every day at a weekly newspaper and talking to everybody about how devoted her brother is."

"And the brother?" Doctor said.

"What?"

"The brother in the New York City morgue, dead of multiple knife wounds he received in a prostitute's bedroom: is that what you consider turning out fine?"

"If it turns out the way I think it may, that he tangled with Mack that night, and maybe just had to fight him off Rita, I'll bet they give him a hero's funeral in Libertytown. Doctor, would you have recommended that she go someplace, like a rehabilitation center, you know, a halfway house, before trying to go all the way home? You don't have to tell me, but it sounds like you."

"I did."

"That's what I figured. Well, the police are going to find her if there's some particular place you recommended."

"Good."

"I don't think it's good at all. I'd like to be able . . . I mean, I'd like to see . . . All right, I'll say it the way I started: I'd like to be able to solve what happened to Pete before she surfaces. Maybe that way she'd still have a chance to get out of The Life at least."

"She ought to return to New York of her own accord."

"Maybe she doesn't know what happened. How about that, Doctor? After all, Pete wasn't exactly an international figure, and if she's in some kind of nunnery . . ."

"You would like to be able to solve the crime before she surfaces," Doctor said. "Shall we go into that?"

"Okay. It sounds arrogant, but . . ."

Doctor Callahan interrupted, "Isn't the word *surface* often used in a political context these days for someone who has been underground?"

"Yes, but I didn't mean it that way. I use words that exaggerate my meaning."

"Why?"

"To get more attention."

"So there was no political connotation when you used the word *surface?*"

"Well, Doctor, if sex is politics . . ."

"Sex is not politics. Sex is sex, although undoubtedly it is used as a means to political as well as any number of other ends."

"Okay, but politics wasn't what I had in mind. I mean she's bright enough, but she isn't old enough . . ."

"Where did the third-world diplomat business come from?"

"That was fantasy. She made it up."

"Fantasy proceeds from awareness."

"I was just thinking, sixteen's how old I was when I went on that peace march I'm always talking about."

"She told you she was sixteen?"

"Going on seventeen, she said."

"And you believed her, of course."

"Actually, I thought she was even younger."

"Which pleased her even more."

"I guess it did. She said she'd been away from home for over a year which I figured was supposed to make me think she'd had a lot of life experience."

"Or to shock you with the extent of her life experience—for one so young?"

"Could be," Julie said.

"Why would she want to make that particular impression on you?"

"I don't know. It would turn most people off."

"That's right," the doctor said.

"And I don't think she could read me all that well. It even turned me off a little when you come right down to it. Which would not have been what she wanted at all. Would it be some kind of masochism, some kind of self-punishment?"

"Couldn't it be simpler than that? What was your main, overall impression of her?"

"I've got to say it again, how young she was."

"Yes?"

147

"Hey, maybe she isn't that young at all, is that what you mean? Maybe she's some kind of Peter Pan who isn't ever going to grow up. Doctor?"

"I think there is a distinct possibility that she is rather older than she wanted us to believe."

"Oh, boy . . . That throws the merry-go-round into reverse."

"It is only conjecture on my part," Doctor said.

"I wonder how old that little brother is she bought the teddy bear for. She did buy a teddy bear on Thursday, and she did go to the bus station about five o'clock. Nobody knows if she took a bus."

"Did she purchase a ticket?"

"I don't think the police know that either. Did she tell you about the brother?"

"Yes."

"Did she tell you he was retarded?"

Doctor was slow to answer. "No."

"I think she made that up too—at the thrift shop. It's run for the benefit of severely retarded children. What a put-on. Rita, I mean."

"I've been put on many times," Doctor said. She changed position and the chair creaked. "Have you written to your husband?"

"Twelve pages, single spaced. From the day I moved into Forty-fourth Street. He already knows about my interest in the Tarot. I didn't tell him you'd fired me. That's about the only thing I didn't tell him."

"Why not?"

"Because I think you made a mistake, and I don't see why he has to know it."

Doctor laughed aloud, one of her rare comments. She brought her chair upright. "All right. Friday as usual."

"There's a lot I've found out about Pete that I didn't get to tell you."

"I'm not sure it belongs here," Doctor said.

"But it does, if I do."

"Then we'll go into it next time, and into why you think it does belong here. What about Paris?"

"If this adds up the way I think, Paris could be awfully

148

important to me. Have you noticed, Doctor? I'm not just drifting."

"I have noticed."

"In fact I'm working very hard."

"Good," Doctor said, without even a touch of skepticism in her voice.

Julie said, "I make a copy for myself of everything I write to Jeff. It's a kind of log. Would you like it if I made you a copy?"

"Perhaps you had better, since you're determined to involve me." Doctor sounded fairly cheerful about it. At the very least, reconciled.

"Wouldn't it be funny if we turned out to be a kind of female Holmes and Watson?" Julie said.

"Hilarious," Doctor said without a smile. "Wouldn't Nero Wolfe and Archie Goodwin be better models?"

"I don't think I know them," Julie said.

"That is the most depressing thing I've heard today."

22

THE ONE THING Julie was determined not to do was to take off in all directions at once. She now carried a pocket notebook, and on the bus downtown after her session she added to the things she had already set down to be explored. She decided then to ensure order by numbering them in what she saw as their degree of urgency. She left the bus at Fiftieth Street and while drinking an Orange Julius realized that she was close to St. Malachy's where, she presumed, the Father Doyle Helen Mallory had mentioned was on the staff. She tackled number seven on her list first and composed a hidden logic to the procedure. Seven was the numeral she considered most important to her personally, and it had to mean something that without her having even thought of it at the time, she had assigned the number seven to Father Doyle.

Father Doyle was a round-faced, high-complexioned man who would have looked like a cherub when he was an altar boy. Now he was forty or so, a little seedy-looking and missing a back tooth. The vacancy showed when he smiled. Which had to be often, Julie figured, since she was so much aware of the missing tooth. He was not the authority figure she had expected. Nevertheless, she remained on guard from the moment the priest joined her in the tiny square parlor furnished with chairs about as comfortable as Early Inquisition.

"It's a great mistake," the priest was saying, "to think the church belongs only to the craw-thumpers, as my mother used to call them." He gave himself a couple of pats on the chest by way of illustration. "And my own experience suggests that the louder the thump, the more hollow the heart. Mind now, I'm not gossiping. You asked if Miss Mallory

150

was a terribly religious person, and I would say she likes to think herself such, a little of the Christian martyr. To be sure, I've had but the two telephone conversations with the woman, that and bits and pieces her brother dropped along the way."

"Being lame and all," Julie said, "maybe religion's all she's got."

The priest smiled. "It's no small thing to have. If I'm not mistaken, you'd agree to that, Mrs. Hayes?"

How in hell had she left herself open to that? "It's not my thing, but sure, I do think religion's great for people who go along with it."

This time the priest laughed aloud.

"What?" Julie said.

"I wasn't trying to make you commit yourself."

"Is Helen younger or older than Pete?"

"Two years his senior."

"Father Doyle, would it be very expensive to arrange a memorial Mass for Pete?"

"It doesn't have to cost a cent when you put it that way. I'll arrange it and you can give what you like. I think it's a fine idea. I've been remembering him in my own Mass."

"Twenty dollars maybe?"

"C.O.D.," the priest said with gentle mockery.

"I didn't mean to be insulting. I know it's customary to give something."

"If you can afford the twenty that will be fine. I'll go and get the book now. Is there any weekday you would like especially?"

"Just so there's time to put a notice in the papers and on the bulletin board at the Actors Forum."

"And there'll be an announcement from the altar on the previous Sunday."

While he was gone from the Room Julie took a good look at Pope Paul. You couldn't exactly call him jolly. On the opposite wall was the jolly one, John the Twenty-third who every Catholic she had ever known considered their kind of pope. 1958–1963. It would have been his predecessor who was on the throne when she lost a father. You couldn't lose a father. He'd lost a daughter.

Father Doyle returned. "How about Thursday, the twenty-fourth?"

"That's fine," Julie said.

"Twelve noon. I'll attend to the newspaper notice and I'll inform his sister."

"All right."

"I brought along an envelope for the offering. You can mail it to me any time."

Julie thought of Madame Tozares and leaving the ten dollars on her table. "Okay."

"Is there anything from a poem or a play you'd like me to incorporate in my memorial—something especially fitting to his life work?"

"He was fond of the poet Yeats," Julie said. "I'll have to think about it, Father Doyle."

"I'm a simple man, remember. I don't speak with the tongues of angels. But I would like to pay tribute."

Suddenly there were a hundred things Julie would have liked to talk about with this man who was missing a tooth and who wore a suit going green about the cuffs. But not a word would come to her lips.

He took her to the door of the rectory. "I'll expect to hear from you by the end of the week, shall I?"

Julie nodded and on impulse extended her hand.

He gave it a brief, warm shake. "Come around and see me any time you want. If I'm not here, I won't be far."

Julie walked along Eighth Avenue and thought of the whore singing hymns; she imagined Father Doyle throwing back his head and laughing if she told him about it. Oh, boy. Now she was romanticizing a priest. Well, Doctor . . .

As she neared Bourke's Electrical Shop she caught sight of Goldie prancing across the street in advance of the on-coming traffic, apparently intent on catching up with her. Okay. She stopped and retied a lace on her sneaker: non-committal cooperation. When she straightened up there he was, his feet spread, his chest out, the cap perched on the back of his head and his very white teeth gleaming.

"You're back," she said.

"Did you miss me?"

"You wouldn't know where Mack is?"

"Now, Miz Julie, you know better than that. We're competitors."

"All the more reason."

"Fact is, I'd like to see him on the street. His 'ho's begging me to take 'em. I got more girls now than I can take good care of. I'm not talking about fresh talent, of course." His tongue explored his cheek.

"Was Rita fresh talent when Mack picked her up?"

"Oh, honey, I could've plucked that chick any time I wanted. I smelled trouble the first time I laid eyes on her."

A police car cruised by, close to the curb, the two cops looking straight ahead, but seeing sideways. Goldie tipped his cap to the receding car.

"You might as well come in out of the cold, Miz Julie. You is just been stamped Goldie's girl."

"All right. Let's talk."

"You're putting me on."

"Let's say I'm using you. I'm inviting you to my shop."

"Let's go. If you don't mind walking with Goldie, it sure don't make no mind to him."

It was quite a performance, Goldie's strut down Eighth Avenue. He did elaborate little dance steps around the plain folks on the street and tipped his cap to every prostitute they passed. Neither Juanita or her mother was in sight when Julie turned the key in the shop door. She put water for coffee on the electric plate in back. Something had changed. Or she had. She was no longer afraid of him. While she was making the coffee, he perused her books on the occult and allied industries. His comment, putting the last of the collection back on the shelf: "This is horse shit, baby. It's got nothing to do with real life."

"Are you an expert on real life, Goldie?"

"If I don't dig it, it ain't there."

He drank his coffee, flashing the diamond beacon he wore on his little finger. It would have been a great time for Mrs. Ryan to drop in.

"What do you know about Rita, Goldie?"

"You in cozy with the fuzz, Miz Julie?"

"The police? No. I'm listening from now on. I don't say I won't tell them what I know if they ask me, but I'm not going to volunteer. And I give you my word, the source is sacred."

"Put your hand on Jesus," he said, opening wider the yellow silk shirt to expose the silver cross.

Julie touched it with her fingers. "I swear."

"That doll is a man-eating shark. I'll bet she cut her teeth on somebody's balls. Her old man's maybe. Or her old lady's. Yeah. Didn't she make a pass at you?"

"No way."

"Don't say no way. That lost little girl crap? That was a pass even if you didn't know it."

"Okay. Tell it the way you see it."

Goldie stared at her, the eyes going needle sharp. It was as though he was trying to hypnotize her. She wanted his trust and made herself stare back at him. The very concentration it took was a distraction from what turned out to be the main action: he brought his feet up under the low table and up-ended it, sending the Tarot cards, the Friend Julie cards, the lamp, and her notebook flying. The crystal ball bounced off Julie's knee: the pain was dazzling. Goldie set his coffee mug on the floor and examined the underside of the table. Miraculously the light bulb hadn't broken.

"What the hell are you looking for?"

"A bug. When you said Okay that way, I got the feeling I was being set up for The Man."

"Oh boy." Julie rubbed her knee. "Everybody's bug-crazy. Where do you want to go and talk? Name it and I'll go along."

"I apologize." Goldie put the table back on its legs, picked up the lamp, and started gathering the cards.

"Leave them. I'm not using them much these days." She had spilled coffee all over her sweater and jeans. "What a mess."

"I didn't spill a drop on me," he said, looking over the golden shirt and cream-colored slacks.

"You bastard."

"That's what all my girls say, but they love me. Now I got three more moving in. They don't figure Mack to be around for a while. Want to change your clothes? I won't look."

"Oh, shit," Julie said. She got her coat and put it on. It was chilly in the shop anyway.

"Did you hear what I said, Miz Julie? I got three of Mack's girls, Rita's wife-in-laws. Now the funny thing is all of them act like she was Jesus's little lamb. Except maybe one chick. Could be that one's stooling for Mack. Goldie could have a viper in his bosom."

"May Weems?"

Goldie arched his eyebrows. "Julie, chile, you and I are going to be able to do business."

Julie saw no reason not to pass along to Goldie Detective Russo's opinion that May Weems was indeed still Mack's girl, trying to pump Julie for information on where Rita might be. She gave him pretty much verbatim the telephone conversation with the person who had identified herself as Rita's wife-in-law.

"You went to the cops," Goldie said. First things first with Goldie.

"I did. I was afraid I was dealing with Mack when I read the note, and I didn't feel up to him on my own."

"Which means The Man is going to bust little May and screw her for info on Mack."

"Probably."

"Or already has done," Goldie added, thinking. Then: "Won't do him no good at all. Mack's too smart to tell her where he is. He'd call *her*. He'd have to figure a straight like you was going to the cops either before or after talking to May. Miz Julie, do you know where Rita is?"

"No."

"If you did would you tell the cops?"

"No." She wasn't as sure as she made it sound.

Goldie grinned, not altogether pleasantly. "What about Mack, if you knew where he was?"

"You bet."

Goldie played his fingers over the cross. Again, she thought of the polished nails as drops of blood. "Miz Julie, how would you like to go to a party?"

"Where?"

"My place. Wouldn't it be something to get all you Rita fans together?"

"Yeah."

"I'll pick you up at five A.M."

155

"I'll be here," Julie said. She could feel her heartbeat drum out some sort of warning.

Goldie finished his coffee and got up. "Be smart now, but not smart-assed. Just fall in with whatever I say when I introduce you."

"Is May going to be there?"

"Unless she's detained elsewhere. By which I mean Midtown North."

"Is she black?"

"How'd you guess?"

"I think I saw Mack beating up on her once." But that wasn't it: the voice on the phone had suggested it, and the point to the question was a further probe of May's credibility. Julie did not think Rita would confide the halfway house bit to a black. "Goldie, I want to know something: What's in it for you?"

"Kicks, baby. It's like for the time being, I'm straight. Five A.M." He looked down at her. "Don't you ever wear makeup?"

"Not often."

He touched her chin with the tips of his fingers, turning her face one way, then the other while he studied it, or pretended to. He chuckled. "Those 'ho's are going to have a ball."

Julie returned to the back room and gathered the cards, personal and Tarot. The worn silk handkerchief which she had got with them from Mr. Kanakas had been torn almost in two. She sat at the table and buried her face in her hands, trying to think. For someone determined not to go off in all directions, she wasn't exactly zooming in. Yet nothing seemed irrelevant, not at the moment. You couldn't pull in until you pushed out. And the number-two item listed in her pocket notebook was "See Goldie for Rita's first days on street." Okay. She gave herself a half-hour to concentrate on the implications and possible consequences of doing business with Goldie. Who the hell was Nero Wolfe? A detective. A fat detective she had heard of, of course . . . Yeats for Father Doyle. Zooming in. Yeah. She set up the typewriter and inserted an original and two carbon sets.

GOLDIE:
Knew Rita was trouble from first time he saw her. Could have copped her if he wanted. (Rita: "I might go with Goldie, because I don't think I could fall in love with a black man.") So why Mack in the first place? Goldie right—a man hater. But a man-eating shark? Lesbian? According to Goldie. By me, no way.

How do I dress for 5 A.M. party at a pimp's pad? Find out: Rita's age, how Mack got her, where she came from, who she told about halfway house—about me. Why? Does anybody there know Pete? Sweets Romano? No. Might turn off informants. Yes. But ask at end of session. What if ladies won't talk? Stay on good terms with Goldie. He does know *something*.

What if police raid Goldie's at five A.M.?

Doctor, I need somebody to post bail . . .

She put the Goldie file with her original letter to Jeff and turned to number one: Mrs. Ryan, from whom she hadn't heard in two days. Fritzie was probably sick.

23

"OH, JULIE, I was so sick I couldn't get my head off the pillow, and poor Fritzie with no one to walk him."

"You should have called me."

"I might have, but Mr. Bourke called for me to pick up the lamp he'd repaired, and when I told him he came around at once and fixed me a lovely cup of tea and took Fritzie out. You know he's been here a half-dozen times since, and he has to pay someone to stay in the shop when he leaves it."

"I thought he was put out of your building," Julie said.

"They're a dirty-minded lot! I'm starting a petition. You shouldn't be able to put a man out of his home after all these years. Not on hearsay."

"Good for you," Julie said. "How about our get-together with Miss Brennan?"

"I didn't want to ask her while I was sick for fear she'd think I was taking advantage of her. Everybody does. You'd think she was nurse in residence to the Willoughby. She's coming after work today. I don't think I can go out yet, but if you'd stop by the deli and bring something, we could have a bite here together. A nice bit of ham maybe, or corned beef, and they have lovely stuffed cabbage . . ."

"Okay."

"And you might bring a six-pack of lager."

Julie stopped at the Forum during the afternoon and duplicated her complete file on the machine there, a copy of everything for Doctor Callahan. She put a large notice of the memorial Mass on the bulletin board.

Nurse Sheila Brennan, as Mrs. Ryan introduced her, was a plain, solid woman, freckled-faced with quick blue eyes and a laugh that banged around the cluttered one-room apartment. She could change the sheets under an elephant without straining her back. Julie and she had no trouble getting acquainted.

"That's Laura Gibson," Mrs. Ryan said and pointed to the wall above her. Mrs. Ryan lay on the studio couch, wrapped in a flowered dressing gown, Fritzie asleep at her feet, his head on his white, aging paws. "Show her which one, Sheila." The wall was a montage of photographs of theater people.

"I recognize her," Julie said. A long neck and a tilted chin, the tilt of which almost pulled its double out of sight. A sensual mouth. Never would Julie have said she was Pete's type.

"You know what I was thinking yesterday, lying here looking up at her? She was out of her time. She belonged in the days of class. There isn't a one on the stage today if you met in the laundromat you wouldn't think belonged there."

Beauty is in the eye of the beholder.

"When Miss Gibson and Pete used to play scenes for you, do you remember anything from Yeats they liked especially?"

"They only played what they liked, and they played for themselves. Something heroic. She liked the heroic parts."

"There were other things I remember," Miss Brennan said. "She could play a fine whore if she wanted."

"If it was an O'Casey whore maybe," Mrs. Ryan said defensively.

"You needn't be so shocked," the nurse said. "I was talking about playing, not being. Or was I? To my mind there are *whores* and there are whores. I always had the impression that Laura Gibson wanted you to wonder about her."

Julie remembered her talk with Rudy and said aloud, "Her three Bs—Bed, Booze, and the Boards."

"Where did you hear that?" Mrs. Ryan said.

"From someone who worked with her."

"Is that the best they could remember of her?"

"Sorry," Julie said. When Mrs. Ryan went thin at the lips there was no use questioning even her logic which was particularly vulnerable at the moment. She had herself mentioned the affairs of Miss Gibson's youth with something close to admiration. Beauty wasn't the only thing in the eyes of the beholder. Julie turned to the nurse. "The reason I wanted to talk with you, Miss Brennan, I wanted to ask about the time Miss Gibson was in the hospital."

"Julie's a friend of the young man, Peter Mallory." Mrs. Ryan had given up her pique for participation.

"So you mentioned. What did you want to know, dearie?"

Dearie. All right. "Mrs. Ryan remembers seeing someone there who's known on the street as Mack . . ." She decided that under the circumstances it would be better not to mention his occupation. "He's a big, gaudy man with red hair. Some people would say he was good-looking . . ."

"I remember him all too well, giving orders around as though he was the one paying the bill. A joke of a man, but he was no joke to the nurses on the floor, I'll tell you that. Trying to seduce the young ones and bullying those of us with more sense."

"But how come he was there in the first place?"

"Well, now, I do know that. I went to Sister Isabella—she's the superintendent of nurses—to complain about him. After all, I was the one who got Miss Gibson into the hospital in the first place. She said to put up with him as best we could. He was an employee of Mr. Romano who was a benefactor of St. Jude's. Mr. Romano felt better with him there in case there was anything Miss Gibson wanted outside the jurisdiction of the staff."

Mr. Romano the benefactor. "And was there ever?" Julie asked. Then a shot in the dark: "Did Mr. Romano himself ever put in an appearance?"

"He did. And all while he was in the room, this red-headed oaf and another like him hung outside the door like bodyguards."

"Would there have been anyone else in the room while he was there?"

"Not past those bulldogs," the nurse said.

"Only one visit?"

"I think I'd have heard if there were more. You can imagine the buzz among the staff. Mr. Romano is reputed to be a Mafia figure."

160

"Reputed to be," Julie repeated.

"Sister Isabella warned us: reputed."

"That way it was all right to take his money."

Nurse Brennan gave a little sniff. "I don't think it's your place to censor an institution dependent for its life upon charity."   *censure*

"I agree. It's not my place to censor anyone." She did feel censorious, but it was not time to alienate Miss Brennan. "Sometimes I say things I shouldn't trying to understand other things. I know for a fact this Mack person has been around the apartment where Pete was found murdered. I don't suppose Mr. Romano visited any other patients, did he? What I'm getting at, Miss Brennan: you got Laura Gibson into St. Jude's, right? It seems to be a whopping coincidence that Mr. Romano happened to be a benefactor of that very hospital."

"For all I know, he may give to half the hospitals in New York City."

"You're right again." But Julie didn't think so.

"Or, there's another possibility," the nurse said slowly and drew herself up as though to say something not to her liking. "Laura was in twice—the exploratory in September, and then again in November until the end. And I will admit, the hospital's concern to please Mr. Romano struck me as a bit much."

"Like they were wooing him?"

"Something like it."

"In other words, if Miss Gibson had gone to St. Vincent's or someplace else, that's where Mr. Romano's endowment would have gone?"

"Mmmm." A noise of assent.

"That's it. That would make sense," Julie said.

"Do you want me to try a discreet inquiry?"

"Not necessary, but thank you."

Mrs. Ryan said, almost blissfully, looking up at the picture, "Isn't it amazing the variety of men Laura attracted? When I was a girl and first came to New York, it was very fashionable for prominent people to have their own bootleggers. There were all sorts of underworld types invited to theater parties and the very best houses. You're not shocked, are you, Julie?"

"No."

Miss Brennan rolled her eyes to the ceiling. And hadn't got them quite back in place when Mrs. Ryan looked at her.

"I'm surprised with all you see of human nature, Sheila, you're so out of touch with the world. But I suppose there's something of the nun in the nurse. Not that nuns are all that unworldly nowadays, God knows . . ."

"It's you and not me that's out of touch with the world, Mary."

Mrs. Ryan wagged her head: right you are if you think you are. "I wonder what he thought of Peter being there all the time, this Mr. Romano. You've never said what *you* thought of it, Sheila."

"We're always short-handed. It was good to have him there."

"But what was he to her, do you think?"

"It was none of my business."

"Didn't she used to call him her nephew?"

"He was more than that."

"I think so too," Julie said.

"Julie was half in love with him. Do you mind our talking like this, dear?"

"No. I don't know who I was half in love with. I mean I still don't know Pete."

"You're just as well then." Miss Brennan leaned over and rubbed one of her legs. "Look at my ankles, the size of cantaloupes. I must go up and put them in a hot tub."

"That isn't fair, Miss Brennan. Please?"

"I'm not going to sit here and talk about things I don't know the meaning of. I said before, it was my impression that Laura Gibson wanted people to think she was more in bed than out of it. And God knows, the likes of Mary Ryan here made a great audience. You heard her tonight."

"I never said she was bed with him, did I, Julie? The poor boy was queer. He wasn't faggoty, but I'd swear on my oath he was queer."

The color flamed up in the nurse's face. "Just lie there and be quiet. You wouldn't know a fag from a fig leaf. Not that

I'm such an expert myself. All right, I'll tell you what I saw, and you make of it what you will. He was an artist, wasn't he?"

"Sort of. A scene designer," Julie said.

"Oh, these were scenes, all right." The woman's face grew even darker as she plunged ahead. "Do you know how he entertained her the last weeks of her life? Drawing dirty pictures for her. I saw some of them myself. I wasn't supposed to, but I saw them. And sometimes you'd hear the two of them laughing, you'd hear it down at the end of the hall with her winding up screaming with the pain it brought on. And I heard her say it was worth it. So there." Little bubbles of spit had appeared in the corners of the woman's mouth.

"Don't excite yourself so," Mrs. Ryan said, sitting up.

"I'm not exciting myself!"

Julie said: "I can put this part together, Miss Brennan. And it goes with Mr. Romano. It's not so awful, really. Pete paid all the hospital bills for Miss Gibson, all her bills, and he needed money. He made pornographic movies or *a* porn movie—which is one of the Romano rackets, distributing them. It sounds to me like Miss Gibson was a consultant. Don't you think?"

Miss Brennan let go the breath she was holding. "I wouldn't say."

Julie wanted terribly not to make her feel the fool. "You couldn't have known what it was about unless somebody told you, and if they didn't know, anybody would have thought it bizarre." One of Doctor's favorite words.

"Bizarre, that's the word." She sat quietly for a moment, saved from chagrin, and then gave a great boom of laughter that startled Fritzie off the couch. "Oh, my God, my God!" She went into another peal of laughter. "And here I thought they were having some kind of sexual experience."

Great, Julie thought, but she sure as hell wasn't going to say it. All in all, she had learned quite a lot, but it was in the area of facts: Russo's department. Sweets Romano, Pete, and Laura Gibson. Well, the psychology of it was over her depth. But there was always Doctor. *Whores* and whores . . . and 'ho's and 'ho's. She was going to be in great shape for her session after a five A.M. party at Goldie's.

DOROTHY SALISBURY DAVIS

Mrs. Ryan lay back on the couch. "Pornographic films, and him at the altar every Sunday."

"There was something I wondered about at the time," Miss Brennan said. "He was never long from her bedside except at night. But he did go off to Boston for three or four days. Now, that's when this Mack person was on hand so much, when the young man was away. Laura tried to drink herself to death while he was gone. I pretended I didn't know what was going on, but I did. This henchman kept the bottle for her: he was in and out the room twenty times a day. I suppose it was concerned with the film that Mr. Mallory went, and if he did it for the money, God knows he soon needed it. She died within the week and the bills were enormous."

"And didn't he give her a lovely funeral? At St. Malachy's. You remember, Sheila?"

"Of course, I remember."

Julie said, "There's to be a memorial Mass for Pete at St. Malachy's on the twenty-fourth."

"That would be Father Doyle who arranged it," Mrs. Ryan said with the certainty of felt truth. "You'll like him, Julie, and maybe you ought to go see him yourself. About your own father."

"What?"

"I've been thinking a lot about what you told me." She turned to Miss Brennan and said, "Excuse me, Sheila. It's a confidence Julie confided to me."

"According to the church, I'm an illegitimate child," Julie said. All right.

Mrs. Ryan went on persuasively. "Father Doyle is the Hound of Heaven when it comes to tracking down men and making them face up to their responsibilities. Think about it. You might feel better just knowing."

"I might."

Fritzie was scratching at the door, a welcome sound. "Shall I take the dog for a walk, Mrs. Ryan? Then I have to go." She shook hands with Miss Brennan and thanked her.

"You didn't mind my saying that?" Mrs. Ryan, the dog's leash in her hand, detained Julie by not giving it to her right away.

"No. I didn't even mind saying my lines."

Mrs. Ryan pulled her down and kissed her cheek. The woman smelled of beer and dentures and tired perfume. "You're a funny, brave little thing," she said.

Poor old Fritzie, all sniff and belly, and not enough holy water left to sprinkle his domain. She walked him on Eighth Avenue, her own prelude. Twilight. The Twilight Zone. In Boston "the street" was the Combat Zone. Why Boston, Pete? Why anything? She had thought she would know herself, knowing Pete. But getting to know Pete wasn't any easier. Maybe knowing herself, she'd know Pete. How about that? The Manhattan Hotel: dark, out of business, hundreds of rooms with empty beds, dusty mattresses, and a lobby with a moving stairway that had come to a halt. You heard all the time of streets that were dying, neighborhoods, but here you saw it happening. Building after building with life at the top snuffed out, sex pads and parlors on the second floors, a few cultists, and occultists selling shabby dreams that wouldn't last the night, sex for men who didn't want women . . . Yeah, even those buying the female bodies of women who didn't want men. The people who were going somewhere went quickly, blindly, mostly to theater, respectable people, like Jeff's friends, with whom she just couldn't identify. What were her father's friends like? She could hardly remember her mother's friends. What did it mean, this obsession with the street, with life at the bottom? There wasn't a thing she could fix. Not really. She kept telling herself she cared that Rita make it out of The Life. But if that's what it all was about, why didn't she care more for Rita? Gut caring. For whom did she gut care? Julie? Yes. Or why hang around? It wasn't just to see what happened. No, sir. She wanted in on the action. Absolutely. But what action?

She delivered Fritzie back to Mrs. Ryan who, having thanked her, then said, "Julie, wouldn't you like a nice game of whist? Mrs. Russo's coming over and Sheila said she'd come down as soon as she gets out of her clothes."

"Can't," Julie said, and it was the only word she could say on the subject.

On the street again, debating between the subway and her feet, Julie was struck with the idea that from Columbus

Circle to where she stood, there wasn't a church on Eighth Avenue. On the side streets were all varieties, but not on the street itself. Could that be the reason the street was dying? Just to see how far she would have to go to come to one, she walked. Nobody said God was dead anymore. Or even that he was alive and well someplace else. It had been a great line when she was in college.

Passing Penn Station without having come on a church, she turned east on Thirty-first Street. In there somewhere the Franciscans had staked out a mission where they could go around in their long skirts and bare sandaled feet. It was the bare feet that had drawn her in the first time. But on the busy steps of the church she remembered that inside there was a figure as large as life—or death—under glass. People prayed there as they did in Europe and waited in line to touch. She had touched Pete. There ought to have been a miracle, but there wasn't. There had only been herself.

Home, she read a letter from Jeff written before she had sent him her long log. He did not even mention Paris. Not one word. She checked the date to see if this one had been written earlier and delayed. Not at all. Jeff was being Jeff, going on ahead. His little girl could catch up or not, but she'd have to do the running. It was one of his Olympian letters which she hated anyway, a cross between Ben Franklin and Polonius. Balonius. "Just remember, you are now that marvelous age which people from now on will remind you you aren't anymore." She'd have to work that one out with a slide rule.

She cleaned house furiously, bathed, and dressed in a change of clothes but not of costume. Whatever she was, she wanted to be the most of it when five A.M. came around. Toward midnight she took a cab back to Forty-fourth Street, taking with her a mohair blanket and the collected poems of William Butler Yeats.

24

"MIZ JULIE . . ."

The street was so silent that the building itself seemed
listening with her. She thought at first she imagined Goldie's
voice. A quarter to five. A night of a thousand hours. And
if it weren't Goldie?

"Miz Julie," this time drawn out coaxingly, musically,
and with a fingernail tap on the window. Who else would
it be, for God's sake?

She drew the curtain she had hung on the door between
the rooms and lit the light in the front of the shop. There he
stood, face close to the window, a black god with white teeth.
He was wearing a dinner jacket. The lapels shone with a
kind of iridescence and the glittering studs on his dress shirt
might well be diamonds. A girl's best friend. Yeah.

Julie let herself out and locked the shop door. "When you
say a party you mean it, don't you?"

"Handsome, huh?"

"You bet."

He pranced ahead and opened the door to a white Cadillac he had parked a couple of buildings down, a yellowed
white in the amber of high-security street light.

"Family morale goes way up when Goldie does his thing,"
he said, getting in beside her. He turned up the radio: Barbra
Streisand in stereo. She wasn't singing it, but Julie thought
of people who need people. Having given her the full benefit
of his sound system, Goldie switched stations to Mozart and
turned the volume down again. He drove north on Eighth
Avenue and cruised, crossing the whole wide thoroughfare
from corner to corner, a smooth, long zigzag in the sparse

traffic to make known his passing to the hustlers still shivering at their posts in the chill predawn.

"My God, this street's depressing."

"It all depends who's hustling it, honey chile." His phony dialect.

He stopped in front of a new apartment building on Fifty-seventh Street and gave the car keys to the doorman. "It's a private party tonight, Tony. Nobody, right?"

"Yes, sir." In his heart, Julie felt, the doorman said, "Yassuh."

A penthouse, naturally. In the elevator Goldie did a little dance step all the way to the top.

House Beautiful plus. White and gold. A waterbed and bean bags. Hi fi and comic books. A white vase with gold-dusted flowers, incense over grass.

"I'm home," Goldie sang out. "Let me have your coat, Miz Julie."

"I'll keep it, thanks. It gives me someplace to put my hands." Julie made a careful choice of a chair, the only straight thing in the place.

Goldie rolled his eyes and shrugged. "How about a drink? Name it and I got it."

"Orange juice?"

"You're the healthiest chick I ever tried to hustle. Orange juice. No lace?"

"No lace."

The door opened and three women filed out in the kind of body-conscious sway and swagger you expected in a fashion show, which it turned out to be.

"Don't you all look glamorous!" Goldie beamed.

Two white girls and one black, they wore identically cut lounging pajamas in different patterns, but gold ran through all of them and they all wore gold sandals. Goldie kept talking to them, at them, a kind of jocular praise, and self-praise about what it meant to be a wife of Goldie's who had a big-time designer on his payroll. Without introducing her he included Julie like someone inside from the outside, like an out-of-town buyer. The girls giggled and seemed shy of her. She had expected hostility. They didn't look shopworn. Not at first glance anyway, but there was something. They all looked young, but none as young as Rita, and nobody was really pretty. A little blunt of feature was as close as she could come to it.

"Somebody give Goldie a light," Goldie said, taking a cigarette from his pocket, and all of them moved at once toward the lighter on the marble-topped coffee table.

The big thing about them, Julie saw in a sudden insight, was that they weren't very bright. And maybe that's what it was with most whores: they wanted money and this kind of look at themselves—there were mirrors all over the place —that told them the same thing Goldie was saying over and over, they could be glamorous. For them, pro tem, the price was right.

Julie got up and took off her coat. She'd been running away all night, on a downer. "Goldie, how about introductions? Then I'll have a Coke, please, with a lot of ice. Skip the orange juice."

"Excuse me," he said "I got carried away with my new chicks." He took the lighter from the black girl's hand. "This is May, Friend Julie, meet May in April."

"Hi," Julie said. "We talked on the phone, right? We're both friends of Rita."

May nodded. She glanced at the other girls. Julie guessed that she hadn't wanted them to know about the phone call. Too late.

Goldie said, the cigarette in his mouth, an arm about each of the other two, "Here's Suzie and Lou. Meet Miz Julie. Now let me say, Miz Julie knows you all came to Goldie from Mack, who's got to be one scared pimp if he abandoned wives like you to save his own skin. I don't think Julie's in with the fuzz. If I'm wrong, I'll make it up to you." He took his arm from around Suzie and removed the cigarette from his mouth. She brought him an ashtray and held it. "Me, I don't give a shit about Rita, but I know you all adore her and some johns like to play that way. It ups the ante, and, chillun, you can up your ante any time you like just so you bring the pot home to Goldie. Now why don't you all relax, get yourselves drinks, and talk with your new friend, while Goldie does his thing in the kitchen? Didn't know I was a cook, did you, Miz Julie?"

"Not surprised," Julie said. She was reminded by the delivery of his patter of a radio evangelist who liked to talk about "green power."

Suzie went to the bar and mixed drinks.

Julie said, "Mack had the crazy idea I was an evangelist. Trying to cop his girls for Jesus. I mean are there people like that?"

Lou said, "Honey, there's all kinds. Some even go to bed for Jesus. Know that?"

"I guess. But where would Mack have got that idea about me?"

No answer.

Suzie brought Julie her Coke and then said to May, "When did you talk to her on the phone?" Meaning Julie.

"When Rita split. I thought maybe I'd go that way too, a halfway house. I might even go now, if I knowed where to go."

"Rita was going home. She really was," Suzie said.

"Why shouldn't I do that if I want to?"

"You come from Harlem, honey. Get off at Seventy-second Street and you're halfway home. You could make it for breakfast, how about that?"

"I ain't going just now." May preened herself, looking into the nearest mirror.

Julie tried a random shot: "Any of you know Pete?"

It stopped the chatter anyway.

Lou said, "You mean the murdered john?"

"Yes." Murdered, john or no john. "He was a friend of mine."

"No, ma'am. He was all Rita's. The cops tried to figure us in too. No way. Not with that cat."

"Why not?"

"He don't mess with just plain whores, if you want to know."

"I do want to know. I want to know everything." Julie decided to make the best pitch possible. "Look, Rita trusted me. That's how I got into the picture in the first place. I hope you're going to trust me. I'm not planning to run out of here to the cops. Sure, they are looking for Rita, but that doesn't mean it's for murder. A material witness: that's a different

170

collar, right? Personally, I think she was gone before Pete got killed. I didn't even know till afterwards that they knew each other. Let's not kid ourselves, the cops are going to find her any day now. And I'll try to help her again. But first I've got to know a few things ... like what she and Pete had going between them."

The girls looked at one another. Puzzled? Skeptical? Turning off?

"Come on, kids. Give!" Julie said with all the passion she could put into it.

Lou, the blond girl, said, "He gave her the oldest line in the world and she fell for it. That's why she came to New York. He was going to get her a job as an actress, any little old job so's she could go home respectable."

"And what happened?"

"He didn't deliver."

"I'll bet he tried," Julie said.

All the girls laughed.

"What's so funny?"

"You're hung up on him too," Suzie said.

"Okay. When was Pete supposed to have made this promise?"

"Before she come, Christmas time. She didn't have no money, so she was an easy cop for Mack."

"Then it was probably in Boston that she met up with him," Julie said.

"He a priest of some kind?" Lou asked.

"Of some kind."

"She told me it was the worst day in her whole life she got a crush on him."

Pete had been in Boston three days, making a porn film, something in which Julie very much doubted he had had experience. The word would have gotten around the Forum if he had really been into the medium. He wouldn't have had time for much else in Boston, and with Laura Gibson dying in New York: that heavy a scene between him and Rita there and then just did not make sense.

"Hey. How old is Rita?"

The girls answered all at once, Lou saying that Rita claimed to be sixteen, May something else without a number. Suzie said, "I'll bet she's twenty-six if she's a day."

"You're serious?"

"I don't mean I seen her birth certificate, but I know, no matter what she said."

"How old am I?" Julie tested.

"Twenty-five."

"That's what I am. Then what was the whole routine about going home as though she hadn't been away for more than a year? And the little brother business?"

"What you don't understand," Lou said, "we're all going home—tomorrow."

"That little brother must've growed some since she seen him," May said.

Julie didn't know how she felt—hurt, angry, taken in. But Rita *had* purchased the teddy bear. "I believed her," she said.

"So what's she done to you? Lied about her age?" Lou said. "My own mother says she's twenty-nine. That means I was born when she was six years old."

Julie shook her head, wishing she could clear it. "I'm not with it at five in the morning. All right, let's say she met Pete in Boston last November . . ."

Lou interrupted: "Honey, maybe she met him in Boston last November, but she'd known him all her life."

All her life. The words once spoken seemed the obvious truth.

"You've got to be right," Julie said. She remembered the absolute conviction with which Rita said she wasn't going to escape The Life, that she'd be standing on a corner waiting for the light to change and a trick would come up and ask her if she'd have a drink . . . Maybe that wasn't Pete, but from it Julie could reconstruct a good enough scene in Boston: him coming face to face with someone he recognized from somewhere else, home, it had to be, and then knowing her immediately for a prostitute. It might be the oldest line in the world, but when Pete told Rita he would get her a job as an actress, he meant it, and he'd have done everything he could to help her get home respectable to all those good folk of Libertytown. She could even go home saying they were going to be married . . .

But then why would Rita have said it was the worst day in her life that she got a crush on him? Even the word, *crush*, was crazy in The Life picture. "Lou, the priest bit, what did Rita say about that?"

"Like when she heard he was going to be a priest she was almost going to be a nun."

Not at two years old, she didn't decide that. Maybe a little younger than Pete, but not much. And by now there was a police photo in Libertytown in which Rita could not look much different than she had when she really was sixteen.

Julie remembered one of her first insights, talking with Rita: what you really want is some nice young Bible freak from Iowa to take you in his arms and say, I wouldn't ever do a thing like that to you.

If there were still missing pieces, she now had some real ones. Julie wanted to think. She didn't seem able to get hold of any more questions. She got up and took one of her rare cigarettes from the box on the coffee table. May came alongside her and suggested, "I'll roll one for you special."

Grass, Julie figured. "No, thanks."

May flicked on the lighter and held it for her. "How come you dress like a boy?"

"I don't feel like a boy. I just feel comfortable."

"I see," May drawled. She reached out and brushed Julie's hair out from beneath the blouse collar. "I like you."

"Thanks," Julie said, and beat it back to the straight chair.

May came and sat at her feet. Lou and Suzie were having a close-up of themselves in the mirror. They draped an arm across one another's shoulder, and turned this way and that, liking even better what they saw of themselves together. Julie puffed on the cigarette. Whatever was crawling up her back, May's fingers were walking up from her toe to her knee.

"Cut it out, I'm ticklish. Hey. Was Rita really into this scene?"

"What scene, Miz Julie?"

"The lesbian bit."

"A little fun, that's all. You'll like it."

Julie got a real stab of alarm. A private party. Do not dis-

173

turb. The street was twenty stories down. She flailed in her mind for a digression. "What did Rita tell you about the halfway house?"

May rolled her eyes, thinking about it—or making up. "Oh, all about the kind of work she'd have to do," she drawled. "You know, with poor kids, and go to school with the sisters and church and going to bed at nine o'clock at night . . . things like that."

It sounded real enough. "Did you tell Mack?"

"I wouldn't. Never."

"You know what, May? I don't believe you."

"Bitch." The fingers had stopped walking. The black girl dug them into her own palms.

The other two came around. "Tell Mack what?" Lou asked.

"That Rita was going to split. And where she was going, the halfway house run by the nuns. Sisters of Charity, yeah." Julie was winging it, but she was on the move. Away from any setup.

"I didn't know where she was going. I couldn't of told him if I wanted to."

"But you told him all the same, you told him everything you could. And now that he really wants to know where she is, you called me to try and find out. Yes?"

"For me."

"Sure for you," Suzie said, nudging the black girl with her toe.

"Keep your fucking foot off me."

"For you with *Mack*. You're his pigeon, May. You want to be number one. Look at you. Mack wouldn't make you number one if you was the last whore on the street." Suzie swung around to Julie and demanded, "What'd she say to you on the phone?"

"She was trying to find out if I knew where Rita was, the name of the house and where it was."

"I'm scared of Mack, if you want to know. I was going to run away myself," May said.

Suzie: "When'd you start being scared. Huh?"

Lou: "If Mack'd hit you, you'd say, Do it again. Hit me,

174

Mack, hit me. More, please give me more! That sound scared to you, Miz Julie?"

Suzie shook May by the shoulder. "You finked on Rita, didn't you? Tell the truth for once."

"I didn't."

"Sure you did. You hated her. You know you hated her."

May tried to scramble away, to get to her feet. The other two jumped her, flattened her on the floor, a whirl of pajama legs until the black girl lay still.

"Admit you hated her." Suzie hammered away, trying to pound May's head on the floor.

"She hated *me*. I'm black."

Julie had to get into it: "Then why in hell would she confide in you about the halfway house if she hated you?"

"That's right," Suzie said. "She wouldn't, not to you, to us maybe and she didn't do that."

"I don't know why, teasing me maybe."

It was the day after Rita had gone to Doctor Callahan that Mack had come in raging about Sister Julie trying to cop his girls for Jesus. If there was any advice Doctor ever gave, it was "Confront." You can't go forward by backing off. Rita herself had told Mack she was going, and for good measure, that she was getting out by way of the halfway house recommended by a friend outside The Life.

Julie got down on one knee so that she could speak into the girl's face. "Didn't Mack tell you exactly what to say to me on the phone?"

May turned her head away, but Suzie forced it back.

Julie said, "And didn't he tell you to try me again tonight for the name of the house?"

May kept trying to bounce the two women off her. "I ain't heard from him today. I ain't heard from him for two days."

"Let her up," Julie said. "For God's sake, let her up. It doesn't make that much difference what she says."

"Something makes a difference," Goldie said, having come in from the kitchen. He wore a chef's apron over his dress shirt. "With one ass a 'ho' don't work for two pimps. No way." He waved the girls off their prisoner. "Now you, little black spider, just take off Goldie's pajamas and get out. I want you in that elevator in five minutes or it might just happen there was a terrible accident, like you falling off the terrace out there and turning up a grease spot on the sidewalk."

"Can we help her, Goldie?" Suzie asked as the unfortunate black one got to her feet.

"Do that," Goldie said. "Miz Julie, why don't you come in the kitchen? Smell that barbecue sauce? That's Goldie's own."

"If you don't mind, I'm going to stay here and think things out," Julie said. She intended to go out the door when May did, even if it took karate to make it.

25

JULIE AND MAY went down in the elevator together, the black Cinderella, back in her street clothes, short pants, boots, and a fake fur jacket, cursing everybody in gutter jargon, interrupting herself now and then with sniffs and sobs. The weeping whore, Julie thought. She could file that one with Magdalene's daughter. The romance of the street had lost its allure. Madame Allure, she had said to Pete before Friend Julie took hold, and he had told her she was in the neighborhood for it. She offered the girl a Kleenex.

"Keep your fucking rag, little white cow." She gave a swipe at her nose with the fur cuff. Little white cow: May was the same girl she had seen Mack slapping around outside Mr. Bourke's. Same girl, different wig.

In spite of everything, or maybe because of it, Julie felt sorry for her. "Come on, they're not worth crying over. I'll buy you some breakfast if we can find a place open."

"I ain't crying over them. I'm crying over me."

"Okay, that makes it worthwhile."

They walked out through a deserted lobby. The white Cadillac sat where Goldie had left it, a bleached hearse.

"How about breakfast?"

May chose a greasy joint where she felt safe. Julie took one look through the window, a derelict drunk, trying to get his mouth and the coffee mug together. "To hell with that. Let's go to Howard Johnson's."

May trudged alongside her, muttering still, half-aloud, her invectives against her persecutors. It was dawn, the whore's twilight, a cold, dank mixture of Jersey smog and the riled Hudson at low tide. Julie caught the drift of May's wretchedness as it turned on Mack, not taking care of her the way he promised. Not even calling her. Then suddenly, stopping in her tracks: "White girl, you don't want to go in Howard Johnson's with me."

"Call me Julie." Julie linked her arm through May's and bore her along.

May ate like a truck driver: two eggs, a slice of ham, two orders of raisin toast. Julie had a grilled cheese sandwich and orange juice. Whatever the other patrons thought, those get-up-and-get-out-in-the-morning travelers, she didn't care. She could hardly blame them: she and May did make an odd couple. But when a scrubbed, ruby-cheeked cat pushed up against her and asked a rotten question, she swung around on him and said, "Yeah, miscegenation."

May gave a crackle of laughter. Julie wouldn't have thought she knew the word. Maybe she didn't.

When they were ready to go, Julie said, "Want to talk, get it all out of your soul?"

"I got to go home," May said.

"In case Mack calls? What are you going to be able to tell him?"

"I got to be there."

"No, you don't. You don't *have* to be anywhere. Don't you know that's the first step toward freedom, not *having* to be anywhere?"

"Fuck freedom."

"Okay, but let's go to Friend Julie's Place and talk about what you're going to do without Mack."

In the next two hours Julie got the story of May's life, eighteen years of degradation. Sixteen, and then two years of cashing in on it. She had been in The Life for two years.

"Why Mack?" Julie wanted to know.

"He just whup, he don't screw."

All right. She'd had about all she wanted or needed to know of The Life. Then she wondered: had she just learned why Rita also was with Mack?

"You never did like Rita, did you, May?"

"She treat me like dirt."

"That's a good reason. Were you with Mack when she came into the family?"

178

"Uh, huh, but don't go thinking I was jealous."

"I won't."

"I was still number one, don't care what them others say."

"I believe you. If you weren't he wouldn't have trusted you to call me, would he? And he did trust you, May. You were the only one."

The black girl nodded. "Number one."

"Did the police question you?"

"I couldn't tell 'em nothing then. I ain't going to tell 'em now."

Russo was waiting, Julie thought, waiting for Mack to contact her.

If May was not exactly bright, she was shrewd. Julie had to hide the real direction of her next question in that illusion May chose to hang onto: "What I don't understand, May, if you are number one, why is Mack so anxious to find Rita?"

"He got to find her right away. They could frame him for that john's murder."

"Who could frame him?"

May shrugged.

"The police?"

"Mack don't say. He don't tell me nothing I don't have to know. He don't want to get me into trouble."

"Sure," Julie said. She had nothing to lose that she could see in putting the big question to May: "Did you know Mack when he was working for Sweets Romano and pimping on the side?"

"I don't ever hear that name, not ever in my whole life."

It seemed like a heavy answer; the trouble was Julie didn't know how heavy the question was.

A few minutes later she proposed to treat May to the taxi fare back to her apartment.

"No. Thank you just the same, but I just think I'll walk."

The lure of the street: the early money. She watched May put herself together and then went outdoors with her. The morning traffic was in full rush. She was turning back to the shop, stopping for the morning word with Juanita, when she heard a familiar voice from a passing car.

"Good morning, Julie." Detective Russo saluted her. The

driver of the unmarked car picked up speed, hugging the curb, until they were alongside May Weems. Russo got out, showed his identification, and took the black girl into custody.

Friend Julie, yeah.

She ran the penthouse and May Weems scenes through the typewriter, mostly typos. When she came to the whip business, she knew what she had to do. She was waiting outside Mr. Bourke's shop when he opened for the day.

"Well, Julie, what can I do for you?"

She waited until they were in the shop. "I want to know how to get in touch with Sweets Romano."

"I hope you know what you're doing."

"I think so. Your moonlight customers make porn films, don't they? He's the big distributor. Couldn't you get one of them to arrange an introduction for me?"

"I'll try," he said without enthusiasm.

A few minutes later he had an unlisted phone number for her. "Better call from here, Julie. I want to know what happens."

"Thanks."

When Julie dialed the number and asked for Mr. Romano, the male voice said, "Mr. Romano will call you back. Let me have your number."

Julie gave him her name and the shop number and then said, "I have to go out for a few minutes, but I'll be right back." She hung up.

Mr. Bourke admitted her quick-wittedness. "You do know how to handle yourself. But be careful all the same. And leave me that phone number, just in case."

Julie didn't ask, In case what? She didn't want to know. She had only let herself into the shop, her own shop, when the call-back came. "Mr. Romano is sending his car for you, Mrs. Hayes." He gave the address on Forty-fourth Street.

"That's it," Julie said. The Romano outfit was even more quick-witted.

"Inside a half-hour."

She looked up Mr. Bourke's number, phoned him and promised to call him as soon after the interview as she could get to a phone.

"If I don't hear from you by noon, Julie, I'll call Detective Russo."

"You're serious, aren't you?"

"There are rumors on the street," Bourke said.

Julie walked up and down outside the shop. She thought of phoning Doctor's service and decided against it. She had a couple of hours before her appointment.

The limousine that pulled up was black with heavily tinted glass. There had to be two men, for one stepped out on her side before the car had quite halted. Julie scarcely came to his shoulder. A bruiser, but polite, he opened the back door for her and then got in beside her. Whether to reassure her or to be sure of her staying was hard to say.

It was a green world she saw, looking out the window. A black one to anyone looking in. Sitting where she was, the president of the United States could ride through the city unrecognized. Or Yasir Arafat.

They sped up Eighth Avenue, surrounded by music, through Columbus Circle and on to cross the park at Sixty-fifth Street. Julie noted the telephone in the car. There was probably a liquor cabinet. No doubt they were bullet-proofed. And yet she didn't feel any great fear. Having had so little sleep, she wasn't even sure it was actually happening. Something hallucinatory; a trip or a ride? The man beside her was humming along with a heavenly choir.

They pulled into the circular drive of a new apartment building where, while one doorman opened the car door another opened the door to the building. As Julie and her guide moved along to the elevator, she knew for sure that she was headed for another penthouse.

But the difference: it was like walking into a museum. Sweets Romano was a patron of the arts as well as hospitals. Left to herself for a long time to wait and wander between the foyer, which was more a gallery, and the sunken living room which was a solarium as well, she moved from painting to painting, Picasso to Vuillard to names less familiar, but painters quite as sure of themselves. The sculptures included

Giacometti and Manzu and an exquisitely sensuous nude infant of white alabaster to which Julie felt compelled to put her hand the second time she came around to him.

Her host seemed to have waited for that moment. "Do touch it," he cried, coming down the steps. "It is the greatest tribute. I am Romano." He padded across the rich carpet. Julie thought he might offer his hand, but instead, coming up to her, he tucked both hands into the sleeves of his velvet jacket. She could see why Rudy had called him The Little King. He was round and graceful and smoothly soft looking, except for the cold blue eyes. She could not begin to guess his age. Even his voice, while high-pitched, was cultured and authoritative: I am Romano.

"I am Mrs. Hayes." No Julie here.

"Yes. I hope you will forgive the ceremony of transportation, but when somebody in whom I am interested seeks me out, they deserve to find me. It so happens, I was about to get in touch with you."

"Okay." Julie said. "So here we are."

"I want to share the memorial to Peter Mallory."

"Oh."

"Are you surprised?"

"Not exactly. Only there isn't much to divide, a memorial Mass."

"We must do something more than that."

"How did you know about it? I mean there hasn't been an announcement yet in the papers."

"But an announcement."

On the Forum bulletin board. "Yeah. I hung it myself."

"I am not uninterested in the theater, Mrs. Hayes. So I have numerous informants."

"That figures," Julie said.

"I had in mind a luncheon afterwards—something at which his friends could gather and drink a toast. Would Sardi's be appropriate?"

"I don't think his friends would mind," Julie said.

"Then you will arrange it and I will give you a check to cover. I prefer anonymity where it can be managed. Please, where would you like to sit?" He swept the room with an open palm.

"Opposite that old man." Julie said and pointed to the Vuillard.

As he moved among his sculptures, Romano laid a caressing hand on a figure reclining on a couch. Julie looked at her watch. He had kept her waiting for more than an hour, a deliberate ploy, she thought, to gain a psychological advantage. It was as much to establish some kind of leverage as the import of the call itself that she said, "Mr. Romano, could I make a phone call? I'm going to be late for an appointment and I ought to phone."

"I'm so sorry," he said, and indicated the chair. He brought a phone to her and jacked it into a floor connection. "I shall wait in the next room."

"It's all right," Julie said.

He went out nevertheless while she dialed and, opening the door, gave her a brief glimpse of a library in leather.

Doctor Callahan answered before her service could pick up the call.

"I may not be able to keep my appointment, Doctor. I didn't know in time or I'd have called you."

"Are you all right?"

"I'm fine. Only it's important."

"Do you want me to call the police?"

"No. It's all right . . . I think. It *is* all right. Only crazy."

"Naturally."

"Could I call you later today?"

"Call me at two."

When Romano returned he said blithely, "A psychiatrist."

"Yes."

"And a woman." He had listened in and did not mind Julie's knowing it. "If you didn't want me to hear you, you would not have said I could stay, now would you? Is she capable?"

"For some people."

Romano smiled puckishly. "Or is it that you wouldn't recommend me as a patient."

"Well, Mr. Romano, that isn't how it goes generally."

"I suppose not. I was joking. I am much too well adjusted to take the chance of upsetting the balance." He maneuvered a chair closer to Julie's and sat down. "I do sometimes think that the greatest charitable contribution I might make would be to give myself to science."

"You can," Julie said.

"I meant while I am still alive. Do you know"—and he examined his hands while he spoke—"these hands have not touched another human being in twenty years?"

Julie could think of nothing to say except, "How interesting."

He tucked them into his sleeves again. "I am the ultimate voyeur."

This time Julie didn't say anything.

"Will your doctor call the police?"

"No."

"She's very sensitive to your voice. Or was there a signal in what you said?"

"She's very sensitive."

"It would be a needless gesture. I have only the best of motives. And the police are helpless. In this case, entirely inadequate."

"You mean in Pete's death?"

He nodded.

"They're trying," Julie said.

"Are they? No one has come to see me."

"Do you know who killed him?"

"Oh, yes. I'm quite certain of it."

"Then why don't you go to them?"

"As you said about recommending me to your doctor, Mrs. Hayes, that isn't how it goes."

"Were you and Pete friends, Mr. Romano?"

"You might say I was his silent patron."

"Would you mind talking to me about him?"

"My dear girl, isn't that why you are here? I've been expecting you ever since your visit to The Guardian Angel."

"You certainly keep well informed," Julie said.

"It is one more of the little luxuries I can afford. I could play you a tape of your conversation with that young clown Rudy. The Little King . . . that did amuse me."

"What about the rest of the things Rudy said?"

"Equally amusing, but more out of his style than mine."

Julie thought about it. "I don't follow."

"Couldn't you tell that he was in love with Peter?"

"I guess it crossed my mind," Julie said. "Who was Pete in love with?"

Her host smiled, the saddest smile in the world. "Laura Gibson. But then, so was I."

That was the stunner. Romano sat back and watched her. Recovery came slowly and she had no way of disguising her surprise. "I guess I've been on the wrong track," she said quietly.

"When you get over the shock, you will want to know who Laura Gibson was in love with, and I can only say it was not me. So I have spent half a lifetime in adoration and vicarious pursuit. I backed every play she was ever in and I even followed her around the streets of New York."

Oh, boy. "Was she worth it?" The question was out before Julie weighed it. "I mean from certain impressions I've gotten, I don't think I'd have liked her much."

"Yes, for me it was worth it. I have become a connoisseur of the unattainable." He was staring at—or through—the Vuillard.

"It seems to me you've attained a lot," Julie said.

"Of the *otherwise* unattainable," he amended.

"You mean Miss Gibson," Julie said, not at all sure he did mean her at the moment.

"It's hard to understand, isn't it?"

"She's hard to understand. I mean living at the Algonquin, then at the Willoughby. All the old ladies there adored her. It's a seedy place, really."

"When all this could have been hers?" Mr. Romano chortled.

"All right."

"She didn't want it. She would have turned to stone. She wanted exactly the life she lived, and where she lived it. And so, by the way, did our young friend Mallory."

"That I understand," Julie said. "Did Pete know about you, I mean the way you felt about Miss Gibson? What was the whip business that Rudy told me about?"

"That disgusting young man missed the point entirely: That gesture was ritualistic—out of ancient Sicily, in fact. It was Mallory's ultimatum to me, keep out, and if I am right, it made him her lover before the night was over. At least, that is the way I have lived it."

"Okay," Julie said.

"I don't know what is okay and what is not. Something else this Rudy missed was the significance in that scene of John Maccarello, one of my bodyguards, at the time. I suppose you know him as Mack the pimp."

"Let's talk about him," Julie said.

"He's not worth it, but if you wish. He has not been in my service for many months now. It was all too much." He made a gesture of distaste.

"He liked Pete—is that how it goes?"

Romano nodded.

"When I began to put things together," Julie said, "maybe the wrong things in the right places, one of the big scenes was at St. Jude's Hospital . . . where they seem to think of you as Mr. Big."

"They should. I would have bought that hospital to see that Laura's last days were the best possible. I came out myself in order to make sure. I was afraid Mallory wouldn't have sufficient . . . ah . . ."

Julie provided the word, "Clout."

"Exactly."

"But he paid the bill."

"Oh, yes. Neither of them would have it any other way. So I created a project. Instant money."

"Pete made a porn film for you."

"If you say so."

"Three days of shooting in Boston. The two of them wrote the script or whatever."

"You *are* informed."

"Why Boston, Mr. Romano?"

"I prefer not to be seen in any of the local—let's use the word *studios*."

"I see," Julie said, but she didn't actually.

"What puzzles you? That I was present?"

"Maybe. But what I really don't dig was what Pete could

do. I mean Pete used photography a lot in his stage design, but a porn film—that's a different art form. It has to be."

"Oh, yes, and you are quite right, it is an art form. Mallory was on camera throughout, the male lead. My identification was with him, not Laura."

"Okay," Julie said. The ultimate voyeur. Yeah.

"You are naïve," he said solicitously.

"I guess I am."

"Now. What did you want to ask me about Maccarello?"

"The big question, Mr. Romano: did he kill Pete?"

"Do you think so?"

"Yes, but I couldn't prove it."

"That's always a problem isn't it? Especially for the police. Shall I tell you how my reconstruction goes? You understand, it is entirely the product of my imagination. This child-whore must have ingratiated herself with Mallory—but that is of no concern to me—except that if Maccarello, in his obscene, brutal habit, chose to abuse her in the presence of Mallory, that young Quixote would not have tolerated it for a moment. And knowing Maccarello as I do, I can say without doubt, he did it to the very purpose of angering Mallory, of provoking him to bodily combat. That would have given him exquisite satisfaction. Having said that, I leave the rest to your imagination. You do have *some* imagination?"

That thrust of contempt from any other source would have destroyed her. Any minute he was going to turn her out. Exquisitely. Okay. "But Pete was killed with a knife."

"There are many kinds of knives—a long thin blade, according to the *Times*. A stiletto perhaps? It is an ancient weapon."

"And what was Rita doing all this time?"

Romano stood up. "Well, she wasn't screaming for help, was she?"

Nor had she returned to give testimony. Julie was as willing to depart as he was to have her go. "You'll have to show me how to get out of here, Mr. Romano."

He nodded, but stood where he was a moment longer. "Are the police looking for him at least?"

"For Mack? I think so."

"And do you think they'll find him?"

Julie met the cold blue eyes. It was a chilling moment. "No."

He smiled. "I apologize for underestimating your imagination."

26

JULIE DECLINED THE SERVICES of Romano's limousine. Nor did she intend to front a luncheon at Sardi's. As soon as she got out on the street, her legs began to tremble. She could hardly make it into a cab. The doorman at Doctor's building told her that Doctor Callahan had left the office. She would return in time for her next appointment. Julie had the cabbie wait while she left the envelope containing a copy of her updated letter to Jeff at Doctor's vestibule door. Then she went home to Seventeenth Street. This time it was home, oh, yes, it was home.

She picked up the morning paper in the vestibule. No letter from Jeff. She had just had one . . . when? The days and nights had run into one another. She called Mr. Bourke and told him she was home safe. There was nothing about Pete's death in the paper. She went through it twice. Not a word . . . fit to print. It was almost noon. There was such stillness throughout the house. Like the deadly quiet of the early hours on Forty-fourth Street when the rats could be heard frolicking in the walls and upstairs Juanita had suddenly started to cry as though awakened from a terrible dream. She had cried and cried almost beyond Julie's endurance so that she had found herself cradling an invisible child in her arms and rocking it until, upstairs, the real one fell asleep again. Across the Seventeenth Street garden, where a single tree was squeezing out spring leaves, the sewing machines were hooded. Spring came in winter over there; even summer had passed.

She bathed and set the alarm for a little before two and then stretched out on the library couch. She would not have called it sleep, but she wasn't awake either when the phone rang.

"I've been trying your office all morning, Julie. This is Helen Mallory . . . Pete's sister?"

Julie tried to wake up. "Yes, of course. How are you, Helen?"

"I don't know. I don't really know. What I called for, to thank you. Father Doyle told me about the memorial Mass. That's real nice of you. I wish I could attend myself, but I just couldn't stand all the publicity."

"Maybe there won't be so much."

"Did they find—her?"

"I don't think so."

"Everybody here is talking about it. Her family gave her up for dead, not hearing in all these years. Mr. Moran died two years ago. I don't understand Pete. But then I never did."

"Moran," Julie repeated.

"Betty Moran. The police know all that now."

"I've been out of touch with them," Julie said.

"The person it's hardest on is her brother. He's just started in business, a bicycle shop. They had the grand opening last week."

"She intended to come home," Julie said.

"So did Pete. But he never did. I'm not going to keep you on the phone. I just wanted to thank you. It's nice to know there's someone human left in the world."

"Don't go yet. Or let me call you back."

"I don't know what else there is to say."

"Pete was great, you know. He really was. I'm pretty sure he did everything he could to try and help this . . . Betty Moran to make it home. I wouldn't be surprised if he even offered to marry her. Remember?"

"Oh, I do remember. I surely do. All these years, I'd been begging him to come home, or to let me come out and make a home for him—like he did for me when I couldn't take care of myself." Suddenly she went out of control, her voice high and shaking: "All the love he said he had for me, and what was he going to do? He was going to marry a prostitute and bring her home to live with me. In *my* house. I thought he was teasing me about being engaged. He wasn't teasing, he was testing. He meant it."

"He probably did," Julie said. "Only Rita wouldn't have any part of it. It had to be on her own—or not at all."

"I don't care what Father Doyle says, I can't grieve for my brother. Maybe I should, but I haven't got it in me."

Maybe I have now, Julie thought.

The woman on the other end of the phone began to sob. "I can't talk anymore . . . I'm so miserable."

Julie wanted off the phone, and yet she could not bring herself to cut the woman off. She was Pete's sister. "I don't know what to say, Helen. Pete must have loved you."

"He always said he did, he always promised. Only last week, we were planning such a wonderful reunion. He was going to meet me at the airport and I was going to see those beautiful plays. I've read every word of them."

Julie got the feeling that this was the way every conversation between Pete and his sister went, from tears to promises, from love to hate, and back to love again, or whatever kind of facsimile you could transmit over a telephone.

"I wished we hadn't quarreled. I hate him most for that. He didn't have to leave me that way . . ."

But he did. There wasn't any other way. Before Julie could think of anything else to say, the unhappy woman hung up.

Those beautiful plays . . . pride knocking with thin knuckles on the heart.

Julie dressed as she would going to see Doctor Callahan. She wasn't sure where she was going, but she turned off the alarm and watched the hands of the clock. At exactly two she phoned the analyst. Doctor's advice was firm: she must go to the police with the story of her encounter with Romano. Not to do so would be to accept the gangster's assessment of police capabilities. It would be capricious, wrong, and dangerous not to go to them. Doctor had all the words. She was at bottom on the side of law and order. Toward which Julie felt a strong inclination herself at the moment. Doctor promised to read her log over the weekend.

She was unable to reach Detective Russo at headquarters, but when she gave her name and the matter on which she had called, the Mallory murder, she was asked to hold on.

A moment later: "Lieutenant Donleavy of Homicide speaking, Mrs. Hayes. What can I do for you?"

Julie got no further than telling him where she had been that morning.

"Why don't you come in and talk to me about it? I'll be here for a while. Detective Russo is on his way to Philadelphia to pick up the Morgan girl. She's waived extradition."

192

27

"SOME GOOD DETECTIVE WORK on Russo's part," Donleavy said, sitting across from Julie at the table in the small airless room with the recording equipment. "A street informant told him that she was headed for a halfway house. He canvassed three or four of them in the East and turned up one in Philadelphia run by the Sisters of Charity. A New York doctor had called them last week to make inquiries on behalf of a girl who'd come to her. The girl never arrived at the hostel, but Russo alerted the Philly vice squad. They picked her up this morning, working her trade."

Working her trade. Boston, New York, Philadelphia. Run it through in reverse and what came before Boston?

"Now tell me about Romano and how you got to him. You haven't been carrying on your own investigation by any chance?"

"In a way I have, but I couldn't help it. I kept finding out things about Pete, psychological things, and I kept wanting to know more."

"So you parted company with Detective Russo," Donleavy said shrewdly.

"I turned off, but it wasn't his fault."

The lieutenant smiled and said, almost with a lilt in his voice, "Let me see if I can turn you on again."

Julie had the distinct feeling that she had not helped toward Detective Russo's promotion. "Where to start," she murmured.

Donleavy shook out a cigarette, lit it, and left the package on the table between them. "I was talking with Father Doyle, by the way, and your name came up. Isn't he a grand fellow?"

Julie nodded.

"Now there's a man who won't get a promotion till the Last Judgment." She'd been right about Russo's chances, Julie thought, tracking Donleavy's association. "And if he got one, he wouldn't be nearly as effective as he is now. Well, shall we try to get on with Romano? It will bring us around to Mack the pimp, right?"

"Mack used to be his bodyguard," Julie said. "You'll have to let me tell it my own way."

"I wouldn't have it otherwise. Shall we put it on tape while we're at it?"

"All right—if I could have three copies of the transcription."

"A deal."

Julie covered her eyes with her hands to help her concentration while he turned on the machine. She plunged in at the hospital scene, going from that back to the street theater and forward to Romano's own account of his vicarious pursuit of Laura Gibson and his prognosis of how and why Pete died.

Donleavy turned off the recorder when she finished. "A voyeur and an exhibitionist. He gave you quite a performance, didn't he?"

"Yeah."

"I'm inclined to agree with you that Mack is dead. That's the word on the street this morning, rumor, that's all. But there's nothing in what he said to you to implicate Romano legally."

"I guess not," Julie said.

"Nothing that would stand up even before a magistrate. I wonder if we really have it." He lit a fresh cigarette and watched the smoke for a moment. "Suppose Mack is not dead: Romano certainly laid out the way the investigation ought to go. What did he say? 'The police have not been to see me.' The arrogant bastard. But he's right. We ought to have got to him before now. It's interesting that when the Philadelphia boys picked up little Miss Morgan this morning, she claimed not to know how or when she got there. The last thing she remembered in New York was telling her pimp that she was going and giving him back the key to the apartment. Somebody gave her a beating, that's certain."

"What about Pete's key?"

"Still don't know. He might have dropped it in the fray. If there was one. The two locks are similar: there could have been confusion about the keys. The time comes out well enough. She was seen at the bus terminal at five. We now have a witness who's pretty sure he saw Mack going into the building on Ninth Avenue before seven o'clock. She could have been back there by then. Mallory left the Irish Theatre at six-thirty, had a bite to eat, and called his sister at seven forty. Then what happened?" Donleavy shook his head. "It doesn't seem possible in a building that size that there weren't any other witnesses. Scared. It's a bad scene."

"Who did finally call the police?"

"My guess is Mack—with raw nerves by that time."

"I do think Mack is dead," Julie said, "and I'm not ever going to forget that man Romano's eyes, but it does seem incredible."

"Not really. I can't think of a more worthless member of society than Mack, and Romano does consider himself a benefactor. Maybe he thinks he's saving the taxpayers' money."

"Do you really believe that, Lieutenant?"

"No, I don't, and the more I think about it now, I'm not at all sure I agree that Mack is dead. The street rumors: it could all be a scenario. Mack could be hiding out—possibly from Romano—waiting for the police to catch up."

"What happens to Rita now?"

"Bellevue . . . for psychiatric observation. That's her immediate address."

"Could I see her, Lieutenant?"

"Check with me in a day or so. We'll see what the medics have to say."

After she left Donleavy, she went to her shop for the volume of Yeats and then walked over to St. Malachy's. Father Doyle was out on a sick call. Julie told the housekeeper she would wait for him in the actors' chapel.

It was a low-ceilinged room with a few pale saints in their shrines illumined by the flickering candles. She had used to, with the sudden fervors of adolescence, swallow chunks of Catholicism, only to violently disgorge them afterwards. Longing and revolt. It had a lot to do with that mythical father whose name was real enough on her birth and baptismal certificates; the myth came afterwards. Someday she might pursue him when the need seemed fierce again. And it would happen, but she didn't think she'd ever find him. Or God. Whom she didn't know any better than she did her father. Sometimes she pretended. She tried. And then in anger cursed Him. Which was pretty hard: goddamn God. What had she said to Rita? Something outrageous . . . Sometimes I think of God as one big penis. You wouldn't say that to me if I wasn't a whore . . . Why had Pete kept those photographs? Were they stills from the porn film? My God, that day in Sergeant Greenberg's studio they had been looking at Pete! The male tower. Babel. She slipped from the bench to the kneeler and tried to pray. But it didn't work. Only a little when she prayed for understanding. Her only peace was understanding . . . For peace comes dropping slow. Was that Yeats again? It was.

Father Doyle had not come, so she left the chapel quickly. She would not have had much to say to him that day anyway. But as a kind of punctuation—a half-way pause—leaving, she dipped her fingers into the holy water font and made the sign of the cross. It was something she had often practiced. She left the book with the housekeeper.

A letter came from Jeff that night by way of diplomatic pouch. Very dramatic. He had written it the night before with her last letter in front of him. He started out saying, "I had no idea you had made such progress with Dr. Callahan." An irony of course. He went on to praise her logic and her ability at organizing her material . . . as though it hadn't organized itself. The odd thing was that if he found anything remarkable in her participation in such a scene, he did not mention it, except insofar as it was contained cryptogrammically in "progress with Dr. Callahan." "My dear little puzzle is going to solve herself." All right. Skipping through the letter, she read the last sentence: "I am reserving a bedroom-sitting room in an old hotel on the Left Bank to which I have always been partial. It may not have the charm for you of Forty-fourth Street and Eighth Avenue, but you will recognize certain human universals."

Well, Jeff. Then she went back to read a middle paragraph more carefully.

"I want to comment on that production of *Streetcar* to which I seem to have reacted so violently. I am quite willing to concede Williams to be one of the great modern playwrights, but for my part, I find the virgin who tries to cure herself of the affliction by turning whore an unpleasant phenomenon. Why not enter a convent, make love to God, and get drunk on sacramental wine? I understand whores and I understand nuns, but it's these nunning whores and whoring nuns which confuse me. That way lies madness. Which, I should suppose, was what Williams had in mind. I did not believe Laura Gibson in the role for a minute, and that psychedelic production was designed to cover her ineptness. One man's opinion. But when I was a young blade cadging theater handouts for somebody else's column, I had the opportunity to observe Miss Gibson. She made good copy, talking extravagantly of her lovers, their prowess, and their appetites. She was a bawd and proud of it, but I have come to believe that most bawds are likely to be sexually frustrated, their bawdiness a rich cloak under which they are making anything but love. My guess is that Miss Gibson and the much younger Mallory played lovers for an audience who wanted lovers and then played tiddledywinks in bed."

Julie felt profoundly that he was right.

Oh, Jeff, I hardly knew you. Or you me. That was for sure.

28

WHEN JULIE LEARNED that she could see Rita Morgan at three on Sunday afternoon, she weighed calling Doctor Callahan. Doctor had seen Rita as her present observers had not, but there was bound to be protocol, and she knew in her heart Doctor wasn't going to volunteer. The best way to get her in was to persuade Rita herself to ask to see her. Nor did Julie want to run the risk of jeopardizing her own visit. She had not seen Russo or Donleavy again, and the newspaper coverage told her nothing she did not already know.

She waited in one of those small consultation rooms which itself suggested madness. One barred window looked out on the tubes and funnels connected to the heating and ventilation of a vast institution. In the room was an empty desk and three chairs. The door had a small window which Julie would have had to stand on tiptoe to look through. The attendant who brought Rita was as body-beautiful as Mack, but he was there for his brawn, not his beauty. He said he would be right outside the door. Julie understood the minute she saw his charge. Rita came in carrying the teddy bear.

It was the size of a year-old child. She set it down in one of the chairs, and drawing the other chair close, sat down beside it and folded her hands in her lap. She was clean, she wore a sweater and slacks, but the gloss was gone from her hair and her eyes seemed almost as empty as the bear's. There were greenish bruise smudges beneath them. She still looked like a child, but an abused one. The teddy bear looked the worse for a week's wear, as though he'd been wept over or left out in the rain.

Julie chose to sit on the desk and dangle her legs down the side. "Remember me, Friend Julie?"

"Yes, ma'am."

"I tried to help you. I thought you were going to make it. What went wrong?"

Rita gave a great sigh, a little shrug at the end of it.

"It's funny, both of us knowing Pete Mallory, and not knowing the other knew him. Or maybe you knew. I didn't. I've been trying to figure out if it was Pete who sent you to me."

"No."

"Did you love him, Rita? I did."

Something stirred in the girl's eyes, but she would not look at Julie. She reached out and put a finger to the toy bear's leg. But no answer.

"I've been talking to his sister on the telephone. Helen. She seems to think Pete and you were going to be married. And you know, Rita, it might have been all right. Pete was a kind of third-world diplomat . . . I figured out that you were talking about him when you made up that story for the thrift shop woman. She said you were very happy."

"Stupid bitch."

So. Something. Something new.

"You or her, Rita?"

Silence, but a little clutch at the bear's foot. Security blanket.

"Or me?"

"Not you, ma'am. You're okay."

"Thank you. I wish there were something I could do to help you."

"I'll be all right."

Julie was avoiding mention of Mack. The police would have gone over that part of her story again and again. She did not want to associate herself with them if she could help it. "Would you like Doctor Callahan to come and see you?"

"No."

"She'd be on your side."

"They all say that. Nobody's on my side, except . . ." She gave the bear a tug upsetting him and then set him upright in the chair again. He did look odd. Or else it was the eeriness of the whole scene.

"I am too," Julie said.

"You wouldn't be."

"If what?"

"If you knew all about me."

At least she was talking a little. "I think I do," Julie said. "I think you've been trying to go home for years and years and telling yourself that as long as you could stay sixteen you could make it. From city to city— where did it start? Chicago? San Francisco? And then you met Pete in Boston last fall, of all the people from home you wouldn't have wanted to meet . . ."

"I could have killed myself. I should have."

"But you didn't, and Pete gave you hope again. Right?" No answer.

"What will you do when all this is over?"

"All what?"

"When the police let you go," Julie said carefully. For the first time, Rita's eyes met hers. Briefly, a fleeting hope. "They won't ever let me go until I tell them what happened and I can't."

"You mean what happened to Pete?"

Silence again.

Julie chanced the name. "When they find Mack, maybe they'll know."

Nothing.

"I do wish there were some way I could help you. Why *did* you come to me . . . when there was Pete?"

"Because I don't trust any man alive."

Only dead men? Odd . . . "Rita, did you know that your father died a couple of years ago?"

Her expression changed. Surprise? Satisfaction? She almost smiled.

Julie slipped from the desk and went to the window. All those appurtenances. Phallic. What wasn't if you got fixed on the idea? "Did he violate you as a child?"

"Yes."

She looked down at the girl, over the chair with the teddy bear. "More than once?"

"Lots of times. He wouldn't let me be a child."

"I get it," Julie said. Almost.

"Leave me alone," Rita said. She lowered her head so that

200

her chin was all but between her breasts.

Julie leaned on the back of the bear's chair. He was coming apart between the ears . . . or had come apart and been sewn together again. She could feel her own heartbeat. "What happened between you and Pete in your apartment?"

Rita grabbed for the bear, but Julie was quicker, snatching it up and locking it under her arm. "Don't try to get it, Rita, or they'll come in and take you away and we won't ever be able to talk again."

"I don't want to talk. Give him to me! He's mine."

"Not until you tell me what happened the last time you saw Pete."

"I don't know what happened. I don't remember. The last thing I remember was Mack."

"All right. What happened with him?"

"I told him I was going home. I was going to the Sisters first. I told him everything."

"Even about you and Pete getting married someday?"

"No . . . Yes."

"Which is it, Rita? It's important."

"I hope he's in hell . . . where I'm going as soon as I can get there."

"Maybe that's where you are. Ever think about that?"

"Give me my bear."

"Soon, Rita. But first I've got to know about Pete. You were all ready to go, even the bus ticket, and the bear for your brother. You'd already said good-bye to Mack and he'd beaten you up for it. What happened when Pete came downstairs? You were waiting, weren't you? He was the only decent man you'd ever known. He'd just spoken on the telephone with his sister in Libertytown . . . home for both of you . . . Did you quarrel? He quarreled with Helen. He always did. It always ended up that way. Did he ask you why in the name of God you wanted to go back there?"

"No. He said he'd go with me if I'd wait."

"Then why didn't you wait?"

"I told him to go to hell. *Don't you see?*"

"I don't see," Julie said. She found herself backing away and stopped.

"He was going to get even with his sister, with the whole

town. It was a joke! He was marrying a whore!" Her face
was like the Tarot Star, a two-hundred-year-old child.

"That's your sickness, not Pete's. Pete wasn't like that."

"Give me-ee-ee . . ." Her voice rose to a shriek and the
attendant threw open the door. He pinned the girl's arms
behind her back. Julie turned to the window, not wanting to
see the way he would subdue her. Then she did the one
thing more she had to do: She took the teddy bear by the
ears and ripped him asunder. The knife clattered to the floor.

29

"AND YOU THINK he was being altruistic," Doctor said. "Does that really sound right to you?"

"Knowing Pete, yes."

"It amazes me that you think you know such a complicated man. I think she was right about him. That does not mean he deliberately set out to make a mockery of her. For all we know, he may even have thought his intentions were the noblest. Even you will admit that some of his noble intentions bordered on the bizarre, yes? But as for the Morgan woman herself, she would have had to do some violence in any case, unless the Sisters had been able to help her, to take away some of that self-loathing. That was my hope. She would never have gone home in any case. There would always have been one more man in the way. Am I right?"

"I don't know, Doctor. Are you?"

"I think I am."

"Why didn't she commit suicide?"

"I don't like pat answers, but I do think her murder of Mallory was a kind of suicide, and she did keep the knife— but where? It is too—Freudian. If I am appointed by the court, I will see her. Whether I shall know more then than I do now, I can't say. And for what I'll be able to say then, there are undoubtedly persons as eminently qualified as myself who will say the opposite. It takes me years to know a patient. I hope I'm quicker in helping patients to know themselves."

"I'll bear witness," Julie said.

"Be careful it isn't false witness." Doctor picked up her appointment book. "Now you want the month of June off to go to Paris . . ."

"You bet."

Delightfully baffling mysteries from

James Anderson

THE AFFAIR OF THE
BLOODSTAINED EGG COSY   57315 $2.50

The 12th Earl of Burford's lavish country estate is the setting for a top level political conference and a weekend house party with many invited—and un-invited—guests. The excitement begins with a pur-loined diamond necklace and the untimely demise of several guests . . . and Merryweather, the but-ler, joins Inspector Wilkins in some intricate de-tective work.

"Packed as full as a good fruitcake, including the nuttiness. Just consider: Time, the 1930's . . .; scene, a stately home, with everyone simply whiz-zing around in the dark; murders, a jewel thief called The Wraith; charming young women, im-personations, a pair of antique pistols . . . and a surprise finish . . ." *San Francisco Chronicle*

THE AFFAIR OF THE
MUTILATED MINK COAT   78964 $2.75

The Earl of Burford's latest fancy is films, so he decides to throw an impromptu house party with guests including Rex Ransom, his favorite film star and Cyris S. Haggermeir, the Hollywood producer who wants to use the family mansion for his next movie. But when a beautiful Italian movie star in a mink coat is found dead, the zany houseguests all become suspects . . .

AVON Paperbacks

Mysteries in the Peerless British tradition
from
Lionel Black

Featuring intrepid newspaper reporter, Kate Theobald and her barrister husband, Harry.

DEATH BY HOAX   41376 ... $1.75

In a small seaside town sweltering in an August heat wave, a prankster is calling out the fire brigade, emptying theatres, and stopping trains with phony threats. But his next hoax is explosively real . . .

A HEALTHY WAY TO DIE   43661 ... $1.95

Gorsedene is England's best known health farm, where the rich and famous pay to be starved and made fit. But suddenly, in this paradise of health, a man dies, and the Theobalds discover one patient after another with individual reasons for wishing that particular man dead . . .

THE PENNY MURDERS   48090 ... $1.95

When Kate and Henry arrive at the home of a distinguished numismatist to see his prized collection of rare coins, they are horrified to discover their host shot in the head. Their investigation into the world of coins leads them into deadly danger.

THE EVE OF THE WEDDING   55996 ... $2.25

It is the eve of an old-fashioned English wedding, where the bride's father has decided to throw a "polterabend"—a prankish abduction of the bride. But the bride is missed for a bit too long—and a mad search yields the bridegroom pulling a knife from his brother's body.

AVON Paperbacks